MY EX-BOYFRIEND'S WEREWOLF LOVER

CASSIE ALEXANDER

CASKARA PRESS

If you enjoy this book, consider signing up for Cassie's mailing list, for more books and news!

1

In my dreams I could pretend the sounds I heard were fireworks or drums, not gunfire, but when I woke to Vincent shaking me I knew our life together was through.

"Sammy, get up. Now."

I sat up instantly. The shots were closer, faster, matching the doubletime of my heart. The Carmino family was coming at last.

Vincent shook me again. "Go," he demanded, his eyes dark. He was beautiful and stern and muscles in his arms bunched, bracing for a fight. "Wake up. This is it. You remember what to do."

I stumbled up and out of bed and snatched my robe off a chair. "Okay –" I ran for the bathroom, realized he wasn't following me and turned. "I'm not going without you."

"Yes you are."

"But –" This wasn't how we'd run the drills. When we'd practiced them, we'd both escaped.

"Things have escalated." He stepped onto the bed and then off of it again to reach my side. Why wasn't he going for the guns? I knew we had them, under the mattress, and in the closets – "They're not going to let me live. And I don't want to watch you die." He took my shoulders in his hands and held so tight I knew I'd be bruised.

"This is really it?" I asked, my voice small. I'd lost so much in my short life – I couldn't imagine losing him, too.

He didn't answer me, just pulled me in for one last kiss, lips and teeth and tongue. I kissed him just as hard back. If this was good-bye, I wanted to take part of him with me, to always be able to put fingers to my lips and feel the piece of himself he'd left there. He pulled back before I was ready – I'd never be ready –

"I love you. You know what to do. Go."

Leaving would mean never coming back – and knowing that Vincent was gone. Another round of gunshots neared.

"Go!" he demanded, his gaze clouding. I could hear the fear creep into his voice – not for himself, but for me, that I'd get caught here with him. It was the only thing that made me run. I wasn't afraid of dying – but I didn't want to make his death any worse than it already would be.

"I love you," I whispered, and ran for the bathroom door.

WE'D PRACTICED ESCAPING, like elementary school kids practiced crazy-killer drills – talked about what we would do, how we would survive, where we'd meet up again in time. I never thought I'd be running alone though, without him – but he did. I looked under the bathroom sink, and there was only one backpack there. *Goddamn him.* I grabbed it and threw the ladder out the window where it would be hidden by the chimney and took the rungs on it two at a time. Halfway down I heard the shots get nearer, with shouting – and then everything stopped. I let go of the ladder without thinking and fell eight feet down, into a bush.

Vincent was dead. I knew it. I clutched my hands into fists to keep from screaming, and gathered myself to run for the treeline.

I snuck out the back of our compound, past men already gloating, and reached the street.

· · ·

MY FIRST STOP was blocks away, a gas station that we'd copied the bathroom key for. I let myself in and sank to my knees on the dirty tile.

He was gone. He'd always be gone. They'd killed him, taken him away from me and now I would never see his face again, feel his touch, lie purring against his chest after sex. All of that was in my past – and once again, the only future I had was on my back. I put my head in my hands and let myself cry.

Get it together, Sammy. His voice snapped at me in my head, and I caught my breath like I always did when he spoke like that. Sometimes I was bad on purpose to make him have to use that tone – other times, I'd genuinely screwed up. It'd been followed by a whip's bite enough times that it made my world narrow down to just him from habit. *What did he want? How could I make him happy?*

But he wasn't here anymore. In my head, or otherwise. I blinked and realized I was curled up on the bathroom floor. I didn't know how much time had passed. It could've been minutes – or hours.

Come on, Vincent. Talk to me again, baby.

I waited, hoping beyond hope, and nothing answered. I was alone. But – I looked at the backpack by my knees. I did know what he wanted, and what would please him most. Me, living, even if my only reason for living was gone.

I bit my lips not to cry and stood up, putting the backpack into the sink.

My new life. Here we go.

The clothes, shoes, and wig I'd packed months ago were still in the bag. I put the clothes on and shoved the robe in, right beside several thousand dollars in twenties – which wouldn't be suspicious at all if I ever got pulled over. *Just leaving the strip club, officer.*

Then I opened up the front pouch of the backpack. There was a charged burner cell phone and an envelope full of new drivers licenses. The top one said I was Sarah Hartford, and there were ten more below it, all with different names. Vincent had thought of everything – except for how I was supposed to live without him.

I pulled the wig out and tugged it on, going from long blonde hair to shoulder-length brunette, wishing that looking like a different person would really make me one.

The last thing to do was the only one I hadn't practiced. I reached for the heavy silver chain around my neck and let my fingers sink down to the locket it held. It'd been a gift from Vincent. Oval, small, and silver, not ostentatious at all. I'd never taken it off, not even when it clashed with what I was wearing.

I fingered the locket and looked at myself in the mirror. My relationship with Vincent would be hard to explain to anyone in the outside world. He was a gangster, and I'd been a whore. Normal people would make assumptions, and say that we were broken. Shit yes we were, but what we'd had was good and real.

Which was why when he told me not to open the locket unless he'd died, I'd listened to him and never had. He trusted me. It was a token of his love, and it'd become a good luck charm. On some subconscious level I believed peeking would cause Vincent's demise, and that not looking could somehow keep him safe.

But that hadn't worked, had it.

What was inside? Diamonds to sell? Cyanide to poison myself with? A picture to remember him by? I carefully pried it open with a thumbnail. Inside was a small piece of paper. I took it out, unfolded it, and found a series of numbers – it was a phone number I didn't recognize.

The only thing left to do was call. I turned on the cellphone and dialed.

THREE RINGS – six rings – who the hell was I calling? *Why didn't you tell me, Vincent?* – and a gruff voice answered. "Who is this?"

I didn't recognize the voice. In the four years since I'd been given the locket, Vincent had never once taken it back. Maybe whoever had had this number in the past didn't anymore, maybe they'd been killed by the Carminos too –

"How'd you get this number?" the man on the other end of the line asked, sounding annoyed.

"Vincent." Either his name would mean something to this stranger or it wouldn't.

There was a thoughtful pause at the far end. "Why'd he give it to you?"

I didn't know – but I thought fast. It hadn't been a birthday, Christmas, or an anniversary gift. It was when things had started to take a dark turn, when he'd been out later, getting his hands bloody, forced by the family to do things he didn't want – I bit my lips and gave an answer I knew to be true.

"He wanted you to keep me safe."

The man contemplated Vincent's request. Then: "Where are you at?"

I gave him my address.

"You're way too near eastside. Can you get to International and 35th?" He named a cross-section on the south of town.

I knew about the southside. I didn't want to go there, but I could. "Yeah."

"I'll be there in thirty."

"K." I began to put the phone down.

"Hey –" he shouted, getting my attention again. "Destroy whatever he gave you that had my number on it. I don't care how, but don't throw it away."

"All right," I said, but it was too late, he – whoever he was – had already hung up.

I stood there in the bathroom, swaying like a losing prizefighter, pummeled by my loss. Vincent was gone. I would never see him again, never hear his laugh, never know his pleasure. All of my memories – photos, hard drives, quickly scribbled love notes on pieces of paper – with him were back inside our house, and going back would be suicide. The locket around my neck was the last thing of his I had. I reached for it and hid it protectively inside my shirt. That – and this – the small piece of paper I held, that he'd written the stranger's number down on for me, just in case of tonight happening.

I stared at the phone number, memorizing it without meaning to

– and then put it in my mouth and swallowed it to destroy it like I'd been told.

What was one more bitter pill after a long and bitter night?

I KNEW where southside was because I used to work there. Our city straddled a county line, dry on one side, wet on the other, creating a mini-Las Vegas along the edge. Along with the looser liquor laws on the southside came looser women, some in strip clubs, some standing around outside of them. I'd been both, at different times. Walking towards the neon lights of the Liquor Barns I'd like to say it wasn't so seedy then, but while prostitutes might wear rose colored glasses, none of us actually saw the world through them.

I walked like I belonged, tough enough not to be a victim, but not so tough as to be a threat. I could have jogged to the intersection in fifteen minutes, but the only people who moved quickly down here were running from the cops.

Vincent had saved me from this life. Going back felt like admitting defeat.

I passed a group of people, head bowed, while watching them from the corners of my eyes and listening in case they followed me.

I know you wanted better for me than this, baby. You can't be sending me back here. I reached up to touch the locket and caught myself. I didn't want anyone I was passing to think I had anything worth stealing.

Vincent always knew what was best for me – better than I did myself. He'd shown me that, time after time. And he wouldn't betray me, even after death. I reached the intersection and stood in a shadow, putting my back against a wall.

I just had to keep trusting him, like I always had before.

THEN:

.   .   .

I DIDN'T KNOW the hotel and I paced around the room. Ray was trying to move us upscale and I was one of his only girls who could make the leap. I'd grown up mostly normal, so it was easier for me to fake it than the girls who only knew the street, but that didn't mean I was comfortable. A nice place like this only reminded me of how far I'd fallen.

Then there was a knock at the door. I took my place on the bed as if I'd been lounging there all along, waiting.

"Come in," I said. The man outside used a key and stepped in.

He didn't look like the kind of guy who had to pay for it – or anything else, for that matter. He was wearing a black suit, and underneath it he was tall and wiry, angular and muscled. He had short black hair that wanted to curl, olive skin, a strong chin, and a nose that looked like it'd been broken once or twice a long time ago. He took off his suit jacket, folded it, and hung it over a nearby chair.

Ray would've already told him what I charged. All I had to do now was be me – the version of me that he wanted for the night. I gave him my best casual smile. "So you're looking for a good time?"

"Always," he said, his voice low. He was so handsome it was hard to look at, especially knowing why he was here.

Then again, handsome guys could be dicks. They were used to getting their own way.

"How do you want it to go?" I asked, pushing a leg out, letting my skirt ride up an inch as I promised him things with my eyes.

"I want it with these," he said, reaching behind him.

I tensed. Was he going to pull out drugs – or a knife? When he pulled out handcuffs, I laughed in relief.

"I'm not going to let you do that," I said, shaking my head.

"Why not?" His face and voice were lightly questioning.

"Because." Maybe on the north side of town, upscale escorts used handcuffs all the time. But on the southside, hookers who went that route wound up on the evening news – or at the bottom of some over-worked cop's file.

He grinned at me, undaunted. "What if I let you use them on me?"

One of *those*. No worries – I could do that. "Sure." I got up and knelt on the bed and pointed at the mattress. "Get on the bed, nasty boy," I said, trying to dredge up some sincerity for the occasion.

He laughed. It was awkward and strange. Most johns didn't laugh when they were on the clock. But it wasn't threatening. It was the sort of laugh that made me want to laugh back, with him. I stared at him, not sure if that was okay, or how I should be.

"I'll use them," he promised, "but don't worry, I'll still be the one doing all the talking." He moved to the other side of the bed, lay down fully clothed, and proceeded to chain his wrists through the headboard.

I watched him like a confused dog, tilting my head from side to side. When he was done, he looked at me. His eyes were an intense brown, and his gaze made me more uncomfortable than the room had, like he wasn't just looking at me, but reading me. "Help me take off my pants?" he suggested, the corners of his lips lifting.

I sat there for a moment, studying him back. I couldn't help myself from asking, "What's to stop me from just stealing your wallet?"

He laughed again. "Well, my wallet's in the back pocket. So're the keys to these." He shook the cuffs over his head.

I knelt beside him, cautiously. He could still kick me or something, right? He watched me just as carefully – he had something planned, and I didn't like that. I could see the outline of his erection, straining against his suit pants. But I reached for his belt and followed it with both hands to his taut ass and sank my hands into his pockets, pulling out keys, wallet, and condoms.

"See?" he said. I opened his wallet up, out of habit. So many twenties – had he already paid Ray? "So you can either take the wallet now – or you can stay."

The part of me that was used to living on the southside, never taking anything for granted, and always assuming the worst was screaming *take the wallet and run!* Ray might beat me, but he'd never know how much I'd stolen if I hid it from him fast enough.

But the part of me that knew about hotel rooms that had not only soap but sewing kits and mouthwash, the part of me that remembered wanting men that looked like this, was the one that spoke.

"Stay and what?"

"Use me until you come."

I sank back on my heels a little. "Come on. I probably get more dick than you get pussy. And yours is supposed to be more magical than all of this cash?" I said, waving his own wallet in front of him.

He was undaunted. "The only thing I want is to see you come."

"I come for all my guys –" I started.

He cut me off. "Sure you do."

I frowned down at him. He was so confident so – what was the term? Cocksure. I snorted. But who knew how hard it'd be to hail a cab from here that'd take me back to my side of town again, and not just drive off when they heard the street name? And I didn't like getting hit by Ray –

So what would it hurt I if did use him? I'd been used often enough. What was the harm in taking my turn and do some using?

I looked down at him again and found him watching me. "We'll see."

He nodded.

I folded the leather of his belt back and undid the latch that kept his slacks smooth, then reached for the top of his fly.

I moved my hand fractionally, undoing the zipper tine by tine, unwrapping him like he was a present. I reached inside his pants and felt him underneath the thin cotton that kept him bound. Then I went for the waist band of everything together. "Help me?" I asked, giving him a look.

"Of course," he said, raising his hips so that I could pull his slacks and boxers down.

I reached for one of the condoms on the bed and unwrapped it expertly, then reached out to touch him. His cock was hard and warm and the equal of any one I'd ever seen – which was, two years into this for me, saying a lot. I slid the condom over him and then straddled him with my knees, pulling up my skirt.

There was always something feral seeming about squatting on

top of a man – which was one of the reasons I liked it. I lowered myself – not wearing underwear was one of the few perks of my job – until my pussy was right over his still hard dick, and I slid him in.

Either the condom had lube, or the tone of his voice – like he was used to giving orders and being listened to – had made me a little wet. I settled myself down and the sound I made as he fit inside me wasn't fake.

I looked to him for what he wanted to happen next.

"You don't believe me, do you?" he said.

I shook my head.

A wicked smile crossed his beautiful face. "Use me like a fuck toy," he repeated. "I'm paying you to be happy. Nothing fake. And don't think you can pretend. I can see you – and I can feel you."

I stared down at him, with his cock hard inside. I'd never had a john like this before – and I had to admit the him-being-crazy thing made him hotter. I rose up, experimentally, made him move inside me, and saw his eyes close in brief contentment, like a cat.

I'd just fuck him until he came and all of this would be through.

I leaned forward, putting my hands by his shoulders, so I could ride my hips up and down. "Is this what you wanted?" I asked him, taking him inside me again.

"You already know what I want," he answered me, and closed his eyes.

What a strange kink this was, finding poor hookers to pay to fuck you until they came, thinking you were like some perverted Santa Claus. But whatever it took for him to get off. And as for me getting off – his cock would do just fine.

I rocked back on him and groaned, sitting up almost straight, feeling him fill me, grinding my clit against his stomach's flatness. He moaned – and I could see the outline of his triceps bulging against his dress shirt – maybe his arms wanted to grab hold of me and take control, to make me fuck his dick how he wanted to be fucked.

But too bad. This was my ride now. I licked my fingers and sent them down to rub myself, pulsing my ass against his thighs to make his cock rub me the same.

His eyes opened and looked up.

"Is this what you want to see?" I opened my mouth and pulled my skirt higher so he knew where my hand was.

"If looking helps you out," he said, one eyebrow quirked.

I snorted and closed my own eyes, riding him in long smooth strokes, feeling all of him, and deep inside my pussy began to clench. I brought my free hand up across my chest to hold my right breast and pinch it's nipple through my tank top. I moaned and beneath me he moaned, feeling things tighten and change, leaning over so that his cock rubbed me just right, my fingers slippery on my clit –

I gasped out, once, twice, and came like I always did.

The 'orgasms' I had for johns were shouting, thrashing shows, but when I really came I did it for myself, hissing and panting, like I'd touched something that burned that I couldn't let go of. I writhed and rocked and whimpered and hissed and felt him groan below me at seeing me come, and feeling me massage him. I moved my hands out to hold myself and stayed squatting above.

"There. Happy now?"

"Very," he said, staring up.

"What...about you?" I asked him. He hadn't come.

"You can use those keys to unlock me now." He looked over at them on the bed.

"But –"

"Don't make me repeat myself," he quietly warned. That voice – it was all southside, what I was used to. I got off of him and reached for the keys, unlocking him quickly.

He took the condom off with one hand and stood, tucking himself back inside his pants.

"You'll come in time to learn you can always trust what I say," he said as he refastened his belt. I nodded, because I didn't know what else to do.

"This is your thing? Confusing prostitutes?"

"No." He threw the condom away, and put the cuffs in his back pocket. "My thing is finding interesting people and fucking them."

"Am I interesting?" I hated myself for asking it half-a-second too late.

"Oh yes." He put his hand out – and I handed his wallet over to him. He opened it and took the rest of the cash out and gave it to me.

"I work for the family," he said, by way of explanation. "Same time, next week?"

I nodded again.

He waited for a moment, looking down at me appraisingly. "Good. But next time you're going to let me use the cuffs on you."

Now:

A CAR SLOWED, and I looked up. The man on the other end of the line hadn't told me what he'd be driving. The window rolled down and I started up from the building's side to walk over.

"Hey," the driver shouted. He was shadowed by his own car and I couldn't see him.

"Hey," I said back.

"I ain't seen you down here before, baby –" he said, clucking his tongue at me.

Some john, or a pimp, Christ – "Fuck you," I flipping him off.

"Come on baby, I got cash –"

I turned away.

"Come on," he pleaded. "Come on, come on, come on –"

I whirled and ran at his car, momentarily insane. "Didn't you hear me? Go fuck yourself!"

I kicked out at his door. The anger I hadn't gotten to take out on the Carminos I released now, swinging my backpack off my shoulder and out at him, missing as he drove away. I spun off balance in the middle of the street as he shouted, "Crazy bitch!" and peeled off.

Vincent had promised me that life was behind me – and I'd believed him. And now here I was, just hours after –

"Hey. You." There was a truck parked across the street. I could only see a sliver of a man inside, glowering at me from inside the cab. Without thinking, I flipped him off.

"Hey, *you*," he said, slightly louder.

I stood up straight. "What?"

"Get in the truck." He leaned over and opened up the passenger door.

I hesitated. I hadn't introduced myself on the phone. It could be him. Or it could be another hopeful john. Or a hopeful serial killer.

I would have followed Vincent into hell – but who the hell was this? I wish I'd asked for a code word.

"Get in," he commanded. I hitched my backpack higher. I had to get myself together. I had ID, money – I knew how to get more money if I had to –

The light changed and the car behind the truck honked its horn. The truck drove off, too fast, angry, I heard tires squealing. I sagged against the building.

Had it been him? Had I missed my chance?

Chance at what? What was there left for me now that Vincent was gone?

I stood there, breathing raw, the whole world pressing in. I had to get out of here, out of town, away – I'd buy a flight to Mexico and start over again, somehow.

The sound of an engine roared up behind me. I turned just in time to see the truck pass me and hop the curb.

It was the Carminos – my God – I tried to run but before I could the driver was out on the sidewalk with me, grabbing me. I screamed as he threw me bodily into his truck, knowing that screams down on the southside were ignored, and he slammed the door shut.

I CURLED up into a protective ball on the passenger seat, still wearing my backpack, no seatbelt on.

"You called *me*, remember?" the man behind the wheel complained.

The truck was old and it smelled like dog. He had dusty blonde hair, short-ish but shaggy, and his chiseled cheeks and strong chin had a five-o-clock shadow from at least two days ago. He took the next three turns angrily, looking into his rear-view mirror after each one, before he calmed down.

"Were you followed?"

I shook my head. If I'd been followed, I'd be dead by now. The Carminos weren't fond of witnesses.

He grunted at that. I kept watching him out of the corner of my eye. He was muscular and he seemed angry – the kind of guy who gave you reasons to tip your bouncers when you danced. I didn't feel any safer inside the truck with him than I had out on the street.

"Who are you?"

He didn't answer me, he just kept driving.

"What's your name?" I asked, still trying – and failing – to sound tough.

"Max."

I noticed he didn't ask for mine.

"Where are we going?"

"Somewhere safe."

I hoped safe wasn't a matter of opinion, as he took the next turn.

I lost track of where we were when we left town and major highways. The fact that it was dark didn't help – and that this man drove down logging trails like they were actual roads. When he parked and turned the lights off, I knew we were surrounded by forest for miles around.

"It's up there. Can you make it?" he pointed up a hill barely lit by a waxing moon. The moon illuminated a goat trail up.

"Sure," I said, not really. What choice did I have? I got out and he reached for my bag. I didn't want to give it to him – my clothes, my cash, my ID were all I had – but I'd be hard pressed to walk up the hill in daylight, muchless in the dark. He started for it with my bag, and I followed close behind.

. . .

I MADE it to the top of the hill through some sort of miracle, and found a small cabin with a wide porch. Max unlocked the door and moved around inside, lighting small oil lamps, and then opened up the front door wider. "Come in."

For a safehouse, it was oddly well lived in, with a bed and a couch, table and chairs, all one room, with a wood stove against one wall. It took me a moment to realize that it wasn't a safehouse, but his actual home, way the hell wherever we were at right now in the woods.

Oh Vincent, baby, were you so sure this was a good idea? How could you trust a man so much that I never met?

"How long does he want you safe, for?" Max asked, his back to me as he stoked the stove's fire.

I licked my lips. Word wasn't out yet. Should I tell him? Was it safe? "I'm not sure," I said, which was true at least. He frowned.

"The water will be hot soon – it's safe to drink and wash with." He pointed to a heating kettle. "I'm not set up well for company. You can have the bed. I'll sleep on the couch. I'll give you a bit – I need to check on some things outside –" he said, and left. I noticed he didn't take a flashlight.

I sat down on the edge of his bed. *Great, Sam, now it's just like you're at safehouse summer camp.*

I did have some decisions to make. Sleep in the only outfit I had? Or change into the robe?

I pulled off my clothes and tucked them back into my bag. I didn't have any personal hygiene products with me, but I splashed some water on a corner of the robe and used that to wipe my face. I found a glass of his that didn't look dirty and filled it with warm water, sipping it like weak tea. Anything I could do to be doing something, not to pause or think about where I was now, or what had happened earlier this night. I paced, and found the room smaller with each turn. An hour later I was sitting on the edge of the bed again, lost in my own thoughts, when I heard footsteps outside the door.

I didn't want him to talk to me. I threw myself into bed and pretended to be asleep.

· · ·

I HEARD him walk around the cabin, blowing out the lights. And then, through half-closed eyes and one dimmed lantern, I saw him lay down on the couch, fully clothed, watching both me and the door.

Time passed slowly as crickets sang outside. He wasn't sleeping. And I was never going to sleep again if I could help it. Without Vincent, what was the point? Scrabbling for a month here until things blew over, and then what, become Sarah somehow? And do what with my life – go become an elementary school teacher? I stirred restlessly in bed. Any chance I'd had at a normal life had passed a long time ago – before Vincent, before dancing, before foster care – when my parents had died and as good as left me to the street. I wouldn't know how to be normal if I'd tried. I wasn't even sure I wanted to be.

I waited another five minutes, another thirty, and then I got out of bed and crossed the room to the couch.

"Hey," I said, standing in front of him in just my robe.

"Hey," he said, not even pretending I'd woken him up. He stared up at me fearlessly, his eyes a rich brown, a trait he shared with Vincent.

Maybe it was a sign.

"I don't want to be alone," I told him, looking down, one hand on the robe's sash.

"Okay," he agreed, his voice low, and he watched the robe fall open.

I DIDN'T WANT to see his face, because then it'd be too hard to not remember what'd happened – and all I wanted to do was forget.

I knelt down beside him on the sofa as he stood, not to take his cock into my mouth, but to face the back of the old worn couch, spreading my legs, putting my face and chest into the cushions, giving the rest of myself to him.

I was wet because it was dangerous and a bad idea – the perfect ending to an unbearably fucked up night.

I just...didn't want to be here. Or anywhere.

But if he could make me forget everything, for a little bit, I'd take it.

He made an appreciative sound behind me, and I felt his hands touch me and fought not to jump away. This was what I was good at, I knew it. This would fix things, not forever, but for one brief moment in time –

I heard him kneel down and his pants unzip, then felt him line himself up to push in, and heard him groan as he got inside.

This.

I felt him start to thrust, like I was a different person, not even there, the part of me that'd run away tonight lifting up, floating over-head, leaving behind just my fucking body, the one I wanted him to roughly take. I moaned as he made his next stroke, felt the push of his weight shove me, making my breasts pull against the short nap of his couch's upholstery. I spread my knees wider so he could get in deep, deeper the better, the more I could forget.

He didn't take liberties with my body, or try to kiss me, it was as if he knew my pussy was the only place I'd let him touch.

"Just fuck me hard," I whispered.

He didn't answer – he didn't need to.

His hips pounded into mine, and I felt the length of him each time he rode in and out. I didn't want to close my eyes and I didn't want to keep them open – I cupped my hands in front of my face like I was at a horror movie, my fingers the only thing I could see. His hands reached for my hips and pulled me back onto him, pinning himself, and I felt my traitorous body stir. Times like these always felt like it was an animal inside me, wanting what it wanted, not caring who it hurt. But I wanted this now, for him to fuck the pain away, to fuck away the memories, I wanted to come and for that moment not know anything or care – he held me tight to him and I started, at long last, to fuck him back, feeling him stretch me.

"No," he whispered to himself, hoarse, trying to hold on. Who knew when the last time he'd gotten fucked was, living out here like a mountain man? I didn't care. I was close, and I wanted it, I needed it, no one deserved it more than me – I squirmed against him, his thick cock stretching me wide –

He growled something incoherent and then he threw me against the couch again and reached over both of us to hold the back of it, holding me there with a snarl. It was wrong, I knew I should've been scared, but the traitorous part of me need it too badly.

"Keep going," I breathily begged. "Make me – make me – please."

I heard him gather himself, saw his hands clench and unclench against the couch beside me, and he made a hissing sound as he started fucking me again. In and out, so slow and controlled, like he didn't trust himself, like he was afraid he might do worse to me – he didn't know that worse was what I needed.

I'd been Vincent's girl too long.

I bit a knuckle to stop myself from whining '*more*' – but somehow he knew. He grabbed my ass and lifted it, stretching my pussy tight. I could feel the tension in his hands. The restraint. I wanted to say, '*Don't hold back,*' but who knew what I'd release?

Then he made an anguished sound and caught up, slamming himself into me like I'd made him mad. His fingers dug against my skin, he pistoned my hips on and off of him, it was just rough enough to push me over – I gasped, feeling my pussy squeeze around him, coming hard, rocking against him and the couch in turns, still filled by his hard cock.

He made a sound like he was angry with himself – did he think he'd hurt me?

"It's okay," I promised myself and him, even though I knew it was a lie. "It's going to be all right."

He made another sound, agreeing, disagreeing, I didn't care, and then he finished himself inside me.

2

The phone rang.

It'd been so long since I'd heard it, I thought I was imagining things. I sat up and rubbed a hand across my face, as feelings long dormant woke. I kept my phone for only one reason – for one man. I crossed the room to it and picked it up, not willing to admit how badly I was hoping it would be him.

It was a woman's voice on the far end. Of course it was. Vincent would never break and call me himself. For seven years I'd been hoping – and he knew it. Goddamn him and his fucking certainty.

She sounded weak and scared. Was that what Vincent was into nowadays? Or who? Maybe it was his sister, or a cousin.

I wasn't jealous, but I was disappointed. I told her where I could pick her up. I had serious doubts about her being able to safely get across town on her own.

"And destroy this number," I told her before I hung up.

I didn't want anyone who wasn't Vincent calling me again.

MY EYES SCANNED until I found him, the stranger who'd watched all of my recent fights. He was out of place against the rest of the wild crowd, them in their colors and gang tattoos, him in his suit, the calm in the center of the storm. I shouldn't have read too much into it – fights brought out all kinds, money was money, and people liked blood.

But it was fun to pretend that he was there to watch me. Even when he brought women along, and they clung to his side trying to keep his attention, I imagined I still felt the weight of his gaze.

A guy like that – he was an alpha. Whether or not he knew it though....

I shook my head to get back in the game. I needed to concentrate. I wasn't scared of losing – I was scared of winning too quickly. I had to focus on hiding my skill, pulling my punches, and remember to take enough blows that the men who lost to me thought that I was as human as they were.

"You got this," Javier said, his hands on the front of my shirt, after wrapping my hands. "You got this."

My gaze caught the stranger's, looking on calmly. He was alone tonight and he nodded at noticing my attention. "I got this," I told Javier, and smiled wolfishly at *him.*

WE WERE the headlining fight at the parking garage tonight, and I could see why. The man they brought in to fight me was twice my size in every direction and incredibly sure of himself. I recognized the scars he had from rougher brawls, and could read his history in and out of prison in his elaborately shitty tattoos. The ten people who trailed behind him had likely bailed him out for the occasion and it seemed they were eager for him to earn out.

We both stepped into the ring. "I'm going to bite your nose off," he threatened.

I didn't bother to respond, just stood out of reach and smiled.

"Go!" shouted the referee for the match – the last thing he'd likely bother to say for the night – and the fight began.

The Mountain waddled forward. The wolf in me saw everywhere

he was weak, the heat of the blood running near the surface at neck and groin, the way he exposed his kidneys when he turned, if I felt like running up and pummeling them – or chewing them out. The wolf part of me liked kidneys, *bloody, warm and soft* – I pushed my wilder side back. I needed him, but without the moon overhead, I was in control.

Egged on by his companions, the Mountain swung. I jumped back just in time intentionally, felt the abrasion of his passing hand, imagined how many ribs it would have broken if it landed. I had to do this dance every time, otherwise no one would bet against me, and Javier and I wouldn't get a good cut. I acted scared and confused while I was neither, taking a step back out of the fight like I was reconsidering my options. The Mountain shouted, his men cheered, and he tried to rush me.

The only thing I was afraid of was getting trapped inside those arms. I danced aside, landed a blow on his flank – *delicious kidneys*, my wolf whispered, ignored – that was more of a love tap than a punch.

He wheeled himself around to face me slowly, like a tank. The tendons of his heels and knees sang to me, so nice to *chew and snap* – he raised one fist up, and this would be the one that I would have to take – I braced my torso while making the rest of myself soft, to roll far away, and have time to regather and survive.

It landed in my stomach. I buckled around it, taking it in, letting his energy send me sprawling across the ring – but not out of it. I wasn't defaulting. I got to all fours, gasping, and the Mountain raced in to take his advantage, kicking out – but I caught his leg and snapped it crisply – *marrow!* – wrenching his ankle past where it should be, and he teetered on his good foot, still trying to stomp me with his injured one.

And now it was too late.

I rose, kicking out his other knee with a crunch, then elbowed the soft space between his armpit and ribs as he sank, one giant hand of his reaching for me to take me down like a drowning man. I shoved it in front of me, and hyperextended his elbow. He bellowed in anger –

and fear. I knew the sound well. After that – I let my wolf come out a little.

Shouts and screams rose from him and all around us – his buddies from prison, those who'd made bets, Javier leaning in, shouting directions at me. And among all the yelling, echoed by the cement of the parking garage all around us, just one quiet man. Watching me. Completely undisturbed.

I glanced at the referee as the Mountain sank, three limbs down and bloody. He nodded.

"It's over!" he announced, using his loudest voice.

"No man, he can keep on fighting!" his friends declared. But the referee knew better – plus the Mountain's last good hand was desperately patting the floor.

One of his friends rushed in. "Come on, man, get up!" He leapt into the ring to shake the Mountain's shoulders. "Get up! Or tap me in!"

"One man, one fight, once a week," I said. Those were my rules. If I fought more often than that my secret might get out.

"I can take you –" he yelled at me.

"You're welcome to try – next week. Talk to Javier."

I turned my back on him because I knew it was insulting – and I knew he'd have to try. I felt the blow coming the second he released it and stepped aside, leaving him stumbling forward. I pushed his back, and watched him fall on the ground, cutting his chin on the asphalt.

Blood! my wolf shouted. "Next week. If you have the balls for it."

The rest of his friends were swarming the Mountain. I had no idea how they were going to get him out of here until a van rolled up, and they started shoving him inside, a man to each injured limb. The disappointed crowd continued to disperse while the controlled man whispered something to Javier, who nodded, and returned to me with a frown.

"Vincent wants to meet you. He works for the family. You want to meet him?"

So the man had a name after all. "Why not?" Inside of me somewhere a wolf crouched down, swinging its tail.

. . .

REDUCED TO RUNNING PLAYGROUND ERRANDS, Javier took my message back. The shouts and whoops of those leaving the fight echoed from the parking lot's other floors, leaving us in quiet as Javier brought him to my side.

Vincent stood straight in front of me, looking me up and down. "I want five minutes alone with him," he told Javier.

"You break him, you buy him," my coach said, before leaning over to spit. "He breaks you, you're on your fucking own."

"Understood."

Javier looked to me one last time to check in. He knew the stranger wanted something from me, though he didn't know what that was. He was nervous on my behalf, because the family was bad news – and on his behalf because I was the last fighter he had running.

"I'll be waiting for you. I'll take my car up the ramp." I nodded at him encouragingly and he turned away.

We were both silent while we heard his engine take, watched his beat up Mazda cruise by, and then we were mostly alone, at last.

I immediately wanted to say something and swallowed it. The wolf in me was fast and tough and loved *marrow* and *fighting* and was without deceit – but my human half had learned hard lessons about reality.

Instead of speaking, the man's fingers reached up to touch my eyebrow, healed now, where it'd been split open in last week's bout. It was a strange gesture for a human – for a man – to make and I fought not to close my eyes in response. Him giving me attention stirred things in me best left alone.

"You were magnificent tonight."

"Thank you," I said, my voice flat.

"I saw you take that kick last week," he said, glancing at my brow. "It didn't even knock you out. You move faster than anyone I've ever seen." He shook his head at the improbability of me.

He'd seen more of my fights than anyone else had, excepting

Javier. I'd been playing it close for months – did he know my secret? If he did, why did I feel I aroused instead of threatened?

"You heal quickly. And you pull your punches every fight."

I shrugged, forcing calm. "I didn't want to kill him."

"You'd get paid more if you did."

"I like to fight for fighting's sake. But not like that." If you killed everyone you went into a ring with, you'd get a reputation. People would start bringing in knifes or guns. I was a fighter, not a side-show freak. And if others ever figured out what I *really* was, they'd all come in with silver – right before my pack executed me for letting humans find us out.

He took a step back and studied me. "Have you killed anyone before?"

My eyebrows rose. "Are you wearing a wire?"

He laughed, holding the sides of his suit open. His body was lean, the shirt tucked in to fit him. He had a gun in a side holster, but no other equipment. I wanted to ask to touch him to be sure – and for a host of other reasons. From the way he was looking at me, I didn't think he'd mind, but watching fights turned a lot of guys on. Whether he'd admit it or not was the question. I couldn't afford to guess his intentions wrong and have him fight me to save his ego. If someone like him wound up dead, people would care.

"Do I pass?" he asked, as the corners of his lips quirked up in smug challenge. I wanted to taste those lips and feel them on my – inside me, my wolf squirmed. *Blood.*

"What do you need a killer for?" I said, more gruff than was required, trying to play it safe.

"Not a killer – a bodyguard."

"Why?"

"I'm about to make some very bad enemies. I need someone I can trust to watch my back."

"Surely you know people –" The family was rife with thugs.

"I do. But I'd rather find someone on my own. Someone without a lot of history and obligations. A blank slate."

And someone who wouldn't mind being in the middle of an

internal struggle. It wasn't wise – but I wanted to know more. "I've never been a bodyguard before. Why me?"

"Your work here." He jerked his chin at the makeshift ring. "You're methodical. Even when you seem like you're losing, it's on purpose. I used to run fights. I know what you're doing, luring them in. Playing with them." While he said the words his eyes didn't leave mine. "You must have amazing control to have never killed anyone. Not even on accident."

I shrugged roughly again, although I was flattered by the compliment. "And who says you can trust me?"

"No one. But I'll pay you enough to fake it, until you do." He reached into his pocket then handed me a wad of cash.

I took it and pretended to ponder his offer. The way I was now, I made just enough to get by, as long as I kept my head down. The money he'd given me was more than I made in a month splitting earnings with Javier.

But I was a were – which meant that I couldn't always be on guard. Not every night.

"I'll need three nights a month off."

"Why?"

"Because." Because the moon on those nights would be full enough to make knowing me dangerous.

He tilted his head with a mysterious smile. "Fair enough."

"When does it start?"

"Immediately. I'll expect you to move into my condo." He listed off an address on the better side of town.

I blinked. Moving in with him – it made sense, but I hadn't thought of that. How could I hide who I was right under his nose?

I inhaled to say no, but the cash in my hand was like an anchor – and the tone of his voice like a leash. He knew what he wanted, and for some strange reason he wanted was me. I liked that. A tail I didn't currently have batted, and my throat closed around an eager whine. *Blood.*

"All right." I nodded, and put the money in my pocket.

"You don't want to know what kind of enemies I'll be making?"

As long as they were human, it didn't matter. "You're paying me enough not to care."

"Good. Go get your things then – and get to my place before dawn." He turned and stalked away, obedience expected. I watched the shape of his body that his suit hinted at, his shoulders, his ass, and inside of me the wolf stirred, hungry for a chase and a kill or a fuck. *Blood?* Heat sank inside me, making my balls feel full.

I waited until Vincent was gone and walked over to where Javier's car was waiting. He saw the look on my face and rolled his window down. "High class brawls for you now, eh? The big leagues?" I could see the disappointment in his eyes at my loss, but he had too much pride to try to guilt me into staying.

"Yeah." I handed him almost the whole wad of cash, keeping enough for gas and food. If I wasn't paying rent anymore, I wouldn't need it, and Javier'd always been fair. He did a doubletake, like the cash might be imaginary, and then tucked it in between the cushion of his car seat and its frame.

"You remember what I taught you?" he asked, one rheumy eye blind-blue from his own time in the ring.

"Everything."

"Good." He nodded once, and then hit the side of his car. "If you ever need to fight again down here, let me know."

I nodded, and watched him pull away into the night.

AT LONG LAST, the Mountain's eager friend who'd stayed behind – the cut on his chin making him smell like a shining penny in the dark – lumbered out from behind a cement pole.

"You cost me a lot of money, asshole!"

If he'd been smarter, he'd have jumped me while I'd still had Vincent's wad. But he wanted a one on one fight – plus the knife he was flashing. I grinned at him, feral.

Blood! my wolf demanded.

Oh, *yes,* the rest of me agreed.

The human part of me folded back, exposing a wolf hungry for *kidneys* and *marrow*.

Humans did sometimes see weres – it was just that no witnesses ever survived.

I KNEW it was her when I saw her attack the other car that'd tried to pick her up. Whoever was inside it was an idiot – she didn't look like the other girls that worked here. She was too clean, not broken down enough. Although maybe that's what'd turned him on, made him bold enough to try.

I started to wonder if this was one of Syd's tricks, to try to lure me out of the hills so that he could punish me for coming into town without the pack's permission. I squinted, watching her for any sign – and that's when his scent hit me.

Like when the driver in front of you is smoking at a stop light, and you drive through the smoke they've left behind – that's how the scent of Vincent was on her. I fought not to be blinded by memories.

"Hey, you," I said, loud enough for her to hear.

She glanced over.

"You," I repeated, slightly louder. It was her, right? It had to be. I breathed deep. Seven years without him. Too goddamn long.

She stood up straight and did something with her hair. "What?"

"Get in the truck," I commanded.

I could scent her panic before she felt it probably, saw her looking at my beat-up truck and think about the time of night.

"Get in," I said, becoming frustrated. Town was pack territory, it wasn't safe – she hitched her backpack higher. The bitch was going to run.

A car behind me honked – the light'd changed while I hadn't been watching. I punched the gas, reeling forward.

If Vincent wanted me to keep her safe, why hadn't he bothered to tell her? I went up two blocks, took a right, and then another right, and timed the lights. She hadn't walked far – I jumped my truck up the wide curb and leaped out of it at wolf-speed, racing to the far side before she could think to run. I picked her up as she started to scream, and threw her into the cab and slammed the door.

"YOU CALLED ME, REMEMBER?" I said, my voice low. She smelled like him so much I thought it'd break me. All I wanted to do was pull the car over and push her against the door, hold her there, and breathe her in. The wolf inside me whined.

"Were you followed?" I asked her, keeping one eye on the rear view mirror. She shook her head.

"Who are you?" she asked.

I grit my teeth. Who I was currently a matter of debate. Pack-less mongrel? Lovestruck fool? Definitely an idiot, for being here.

"What's your name?" she pressed.

"Max."

"Where are we going?"

"Someplace safe."

I could tell she didn't believe me. It didn't matter.

I DROVE FOR MY CABIN. I knew of safer places deeper in the woods, but we'd have to backpack in, and she didn't look like the type. Tomorrow I'd bother to talk to her, come up with a plan, swallow my pride and ask how Vincent was.

I parked in the old washout below the cabin's ridge. There was plenty of moonlight for me but not nearly enough for her. I took her bag and led her up the hillside, waiting to hear an ankle snap. To her credit she didn't protest and when we got to the cabin I let us both in.

I watched her looking around, then went to stoke the fire. "How long does he want you safe for?" I stopped from asking what I really wanted to know – *is he going to come and get you back himself?* I wanted that so badly – even as I knew it was an impossibly bad idea, one that'd get us both killed.

"I'm not sure," she said. I listened closely. She wasn't lying. Guess I'd have to keep the phone on for a little longer.

"The water will be hot soon – it's safe to drink and wash with." I pointed to the kettle I kept full. "I'm not set up well for company. You can have the bed. I'll sleep on the couch. I'll give you a bit – I need to check on some things outside –"

Too late, outside, I remembered I should've taken a flashlight for appearance's sake.

I DIDN'T THINK she'd leave the cabin tonight – but that didn't mean that we weren't followed. I went to the edge of the ridge and breathed the night air in deep. The only scents out here were smoke from my fire, musk from my fur, and her – who largely smelled like *him*, to me.

All those years ago – all those nights – blood raced around my body like it hadn't in years, like I was a teenager again, all hormones and hope. My wolf wanted out, as restless as the rest of me. I shook my head and tightened my reins.

I walked along the ridge, listening to the nightlife and for tires, all my senses taut. Coming full circle I sat down, my back to a tree, and watched her through a smudged window. I didn't want to be in there with her alone – and I doubted she wanted to be in there with me.

Vincent, you'd better fucking have a plan.

An hour passed. Long enough for her to feel safe, or so I hoped – and for me to catch anyone who'd tracked us in. The pack knew where I was, but no one else did, and they were too busy to bother with me. I walked to the cabin's door and opened it. She was on top the bed, pretending to be asleep. Two could play that game. I blew out every light but one to save oil, and stretched out on the couch, eyes half-closed, listening to her breathing and the steady sawing sound of undisturbed crickets outside.

I was still tense. What had happened? Why had Vincent sent her here? How bad were things? And every time I inhaled, it was like breathing him in again, smelling him, remembering how he – I heard her shift on the bed, up to standing. She was wearing a robe now, and I watched her walk over.

"Hey," she said.

"Hey," I answered her, unsure. This close – her scent was just as strong as his. Inside of me, my wolf paced and whined, and blood sunk low.

"I don't want to be alone," she said, looking down at me, one hand on her robe's sash.

"Okay," I agreed, and watched her robe fall open.

I stood to breathe more of her in. It was all I could do not to touch her, bring her close to me and breathe her in deep, to paw my hands against her skin and feel the softness of her flesh. My wolf was riding just under the surface now and it *wanted* – I ground my teeth together, forcing it back without touching her. I breathed hard and low, feeling my cock strain against the inside of my pants, praying that she wouldn't change her mind. And then she took a pose of submission in front of me, recognizable to any wolf – her chest and face down in the couch cushions, her naked ass up.

I bit back a growl, undid my belt, unzipped my fly, and pulled out my cock.

I could taste her wetness in the air, the sweet tang of her readiness, feel-see the heat radiating off of her pussy. I wanted to push my nose between her legs and taste the juices there, but that would be too personal – I still didn't know her name and didn't want to.

All I wanted was a fuck. And judging from the way she held herself, legs spread wide, that was all she wanted too. I knelt and reached between us to tilt my cock down, sliding it down between the cheeks of her ass until it found home. I pushed into her as she opened for me with a gasp, and felt her pussy take my cock whole.

How long had it been since I'd been with anyone? Since I'd felt sweet warm heat wrapped around my cock?

I thrust slowly, relishing each inch of her, trying to control myself and the *needs* that started rising to the surface. My wolf wanted to take her hard, to bite her neck and claw her back and – I took the solid cheeks of her ass in my hands, felt the flesh move with my grip, and stopped myself from more. She was important to Vincent, and I would never mark anything he loved – but when she moaned and pushed back into me, I couldn't help but thrust harder.

I held onto her hips in earnest as I rocked in and out, pushing her into the couch. The champagne color of her skin beneath the oil lamp – listening to her pant with each of my thrusts – her skin, her smell, his smell, my cock, her pussy –

"No –" I protested, as my inner nature tried to come through. I wasn't the only one who wanted this – it'd been a long time for my wolf, too. He was clawing at the inside of my mind, desperate to gain control, to *mount* her – and I felt my mating knot beginning to swell. "No –" I panted, begging my cock to behave.

She moaned beneath me, spreading her legs wider, as if asking to be knotted.

"It's okay," she promised, grinding her ass back against me, her pussy clenching me. "It's going to be all right –"

My thickening cock gave me no other choice – I pounded myself into her, feeling her pussy wrapped around it – feeling the quivers of her goddamned coming around me, like she owned me –

I growled and finished myself inside her, unable to do anything but, needing to come before I was betrayed by my own lust. When I was done I stared down at her, breathing hard, fighting to collect myself, to calm myself, to pull myself back from the brink of my wolf's desires. I barely managed to control myself in time and slide my cock out.

Oh my God. Years of trying to keep my head down and stay off the map – only to almost let my wolf mate itself someone I didn't even know.

She stank of Vincent. That had to have been what'd done it, what'd pushed me over the edge.

I panted, gathering myself slowly, only one thought on my mind.

For me it was an imprecation, for my wolf, a command.

Fuck.

3

"I haven't – done that –" he whispered, his voice hoarse.

"It's okay, mountain man," I said, feeling him slide out of me. "I wanted it too." I rose up, shaky, pulling my robe back up. Fucking a stranger. So high on the bad decision scale it hurt. But hurting myself always felt right, when left to my own devices. And Vincent wasn't around anymore to keep my head on straight, or do the hurting for me. I clutched both my hands at my sides, suddenly about to cry.

"Where's your bathroom?" And then I remembered how rustic this place was.

"Outside."

"Is there...toilet paper?"

"I live away from civilization, not in the middle of nowhere." He said brusquely, standing and pushing his dick back into his pants. Fucking me hadn't made him any kinder. "Take a flashlight – it's on the house's east side." He pointed to the lights hanging near the wall. "East is to your right," he called, as I closed the door.

I didn't turn on the flashlight immediately once I was out. Instead I listened to the crickets and felt the night press down on me like a hand.

I was alone. The immediacy of physical contact had pushed the truth back for a while but if I didn't keep fucking-being-fucked, it wouldn't stay away. I'd been in this place before, the dark place, after my parents had died. No one on this entire planet cared if I lived or died, now that Vincent was gone. Not the crickets sawing all around me, or the strange man inside the cabin.

I turned the flashlight on, ran for the outhouse, and cried.

I WAS on the bed in front of him, tied up like he liked, hands over my head, completely helpless. His fingers were on the last button of my blouse, exposing a red and black lace bra I'd bought just for him, and he was looking down appreciatively.

"Tonight I want to do something different."

"Okay," I breathed, tense, scared, hungry.

My nights with Vincent had changed me. He'd been seeing me for three months now, one night a week. The extra cash that Ray'd let me keep I'd spent on dressing up – I looked like a girl you picked up at a bar now, not one who walked in from the corner – but I only dressed up for him. Looking too nice made other johns angry, they wanted to take you down a notch, imagining you to be their ex-wife or current boss, and I didn't like getting hit.

Except by him.

It made no sense, I know. It was hard to explain, and I never got the chance to say what I thought about it aloud, which made it harder. All I knew was that he didn't hurt me like other clients did, on accident, or with anger – with him it was some kind of push and pull, to see how far I would let him go, to see how far he could take me. There'd been spankings and clothespins and I would tremble, not-scared-really-scared, on a precarious brink until he'd let me go. He would eat me out then, until I came, my legs wrapped around him as I writhed, arms still bound, and then he'd untie me and go, and I'd stay in the room for the rest of the night.

It felt like being Cinderella, for twelve hours at a time.

I looked up at him, wondering what would happen next, what he could do to me that he hadn't already done as his gaze studied mine.

"I'm afraid tonight might be a very long night, Sam."

I nodded, a little afraid. "Why?"

"I've never broken you, have I?"

I shook my head.

"Well, tonight I'm going to have to." His face looked resolved, and I tensed. Here it was, the moment it all fell apart – I'd been a fool to look forward to these nights, to think that I was special, that he was special –

"Stop squirming," he demanded, and I did. "Look at me."

I stared directly at him, even though the look that he was giving me now felt like it burned.

"We're at a plateau, you and I. Either we continue, or we don't. I can let you go now, if you want, pay you for the night, and never see you again. Or you can stay and find out what I want. Make up your mind."

I wanted him to repeat what he'd said, but I knew if I did he'd think it hesitation. I stared up at him, trying to find answers in his eyes. Could I trust him? I'd already let him tie me up. What more did he want? My heart was beating so loudly in my chest I wondered if he could hear it.

There was one thing I knew about him from our time together – he always wanted the truth from me. When we'd started, I'd tried to be too brave once and he'd hurt me. I thought he'd be pleased that I'd let him go so far, but he was mad at me for lying to him instead. It'd taken me days to understand why.

"I'm scared," I told him, truthfully.

He nodded. "You have every right to be. Up until now I've played with you, and rewarded you for it. But you have no idea what it's like to actually serve me." He brushed a stray lock of hair away from my eyes, still looking down.

"Is that what you want?" I whispered in hope. I could do that. I was used to serving people – Ray, the other johns – service didn't frighten me.

He smiled a little. "Yes. But more than you've given any other man so far."

"How so?"

He rubbed his thumb across my lips, as if he was stealing a kiss for later. "Do you want to stay?"

I LOOKED around the room we were in – so much nicer than the room I stayed in at Ray's – saw the black lace of my bra against the red, felt the satin of my blouse against my back. But more than all of that, I looked at him, his stern face that smiled so readily, his brown eyes, intense or soft. Hotel rooms could come and go, lingerie could be rebought, but I wasn't ready to be without him in my life just yet.

"I do."

His gaze softened and he exhaled – that was the first time I ever realized that he wanted this too. That he was scared of losing me. "Good." He reached over my head and untied my wrists.

I swallowed. "Now what?" What would 'service' entail? Acting like a cocktail waitress? Blowjobs?

He rocked back on the mattress. "Now, I'm going to make you cry on purpose because it pleases me. It's going to hurt. I'm sorry."

I pushed up onto my elbows. "What?"

He looked over at me, daring me to challenge him again. It wasn't too late, no matter what I'd said – but – I wanted to be here more than I wanted to leave, so far.

"Why?" I asked, as he rummaged in the bag he'd brought, pulling out a wooden hairbrush. I hated that thing, it stung so bad when he spanked me with its wooden side, the carvings there leaving little lines up and down my ass in its wake.

"Because." He pointed with the brush to the door. "You can leave, if you'd like."

Which was why he'd untied me. So I could just go.

Other girls were better actresses than I was, they would've cried on command just to get to the minibar. I couldn't pull that off. "But –"

I protested as he reached for my hips to turn me over. "Just tell me why? Please?"

He hesitated, and let me rock back down. Emotions flew across his face, too quickly for me to read. "I want to see you, the real you, with all your armor down. I don't want there to be any secrets between us, Sam. Secrets only wind up hurting worse, later."

"But you don't have to make me cry for that –"

"I'm afraid I do." His expression was solemn, his voice cold and frightening.

"I've cried with you before –" I protested.

"This time is going to be different."

I bit my lips. "But – you don't even understand what you're asking!"

One of his eyebrows raised. "Then tell me."

I looked around the room we were in – his room, his world, and me, just a placeholder in it – I didn't belong here, I didn't get to keep it, none of this was real – I grabbed hold of the scab that hid what my life was like when I wasn't in here being a Cinderella with him and pulled. "When you leave here, you get to go back to your amazing life where you have money and you do whatever it is you want to do all the time. When I leave here, I go back to Ray, and a room I share with three other girls, all of whom at one time or another have stolen my stuff, and I put on torn tights and a spandex skirt and wait for calls." Words came rushing out of me like blood. No one else wanted to hear about the room, or the way that that life was, how scary things could be, how precarious it felt to never really get to hope – I was breathing heavy now, scared of being with him, scared of being without him, and I was crying, goddammit, which wasn't fair, because it probably didn't count. "You want me to take my armor off, just to amuse you? To feel real feelings when we both know real feelings hurt? Fuck you, Vincent," I said, hands balled into fists, sobbing. "I'm a human being, not a puppet."

"I know you're not a toy, Samantha," he said, his voice low. This was it, I was ruining it, I could tell.

"Let's just fuck like we always do, okay?" I said, my voice small, hoping beyond hope that I could turn back the clock.

He stared down at me, tears rolling down my cheeks, my chest heaving, as I savagely wiped my eyes and my nose with the back of one hand. Cinderellas didn't cry. Cinderellas were tough and did what their Prince Charmings wanted, even when those Prince Charmings held the hairbrush.

I watched him set the hairbrush aside. Here it'd come, the part where he'd throw me out of bed, and I'd have to explain to Ray how come the gravy train had stopped. But instead his hands went to the button of his collar, to undo it. I watched him unbutton the next one too, my lips parting in a silent gasp as I wiped my tears away again.

He undressed himself. I'd never seen the skin of his chest before and I wanted to run my hands over it, but I was too afraid that moving would break this moment. I could see what looked like a knife scar a few inches from his neck, and one tattoo, the pawprint of a wolf right on top his heart. He kicked off his dress shoes and pulled off his socks, and then unlatched his belt. I wondered for a hot second if he would be using it on me, before he let it fall with the rest of his clothing and kicked himself free.

It was his turn to be naked in front of me, like I always was for him. His body was as amazing as I'd always known it would be, feeling it for so long beneath his clothes. Lean and muscular, dusted with dark hair, cut like a classical statue. He moved to lay beside me, lining his body up with mine, and he kissed me.

He hardly ever kissed me. I knew because I'd counted each and every one. His lips pressed against mine, strong yet soft, and his tongue pushed in, as firm as the cock that was right by my hand. Instinct took over and I shimmied my skirt down and undid the front clasp of my bra. He kissed a line down my throat to my nipples and sucked at them.

I wasn't sure what this was, we'd never been like this – for all I knew, this was a good-bye fuck – but I liked it. He rocked himself over me, put on a condom, and slid himself in. I moaned as he fit me perfectly, just like our first night.

"Is this what you wanted? A little bit of normalcy?" he asked, holding himself up on his elbows and stroking in and out.

I nodded. From here I could touch his face and his scar, feel his skin. Everything we'd done before now had been intense – but this was intimate. Even for me, who was so used to fucking.

"We're not normal people though," he warned.

I dared to smile. "I know. But it's nice to pretend sometimes."

He paused and chuckled, smiling back, then kissing my forehead as he thrust deep inside again. I groaned and arced my hips up to feel more of him, and he purred. Our bodies moved together, knowing what we needed more than either of us could admit.

He took a handful of my hair and pulled it back, showing him my neck. "I just want you to trust me, Sam, with everything you have," he said, as he kissed down it.

"What if I don't know how?" I panted. Our hips were tight and things were building inside. My body wanted him – and so did I.

"I'll show you. I'll beat it into you, if I have to." He thrust harder now, faster, taking control. He bent his head down and started fucking me in earnest, and I cried out after each thrust, egging him on, both of us fucking like it was our last night on earth. My fingers clawed into his shoulders as my pussy clenched around him, so close to going off.

Three more thrusts and – "Oh my God – Vincent –" I held onto him, my orgasm rolling through me in waves. "Vincent," I breathed his name out because I needed to, because I wanted him to be mine.

He came right after that with a shout, throwing his head back in the glory of the moment. He sagged over me, still inside, sweat dripping between us. That was the first time I'd ever seen him lose control – and I realized he didn't just want to have my trust, he wanted to trust me, too. Maybe he was as lonely as I was. Maybe we could have each other. My heart thrilled at the thought – and I put a hand to my mouth in horror.

I was in love with him – and it would never, ever, work out. What the hell was wrong with me? He collapsed to my side, took my hand to his face, and kissed my palm.

He spent the night with me that night for the first time. And he didn't know it, but I cried again after he went to sleep – the tears of a foolish hooker in love with her cruelest-nicest john.

I CLEANED myself up enough to go back into the cabin. I knew it was dim, so I was sure to turn the flashlight off as I walked in the door. Max was still on the couch – that was good, despite our recent interlude I didn't want him assuming things. I made my way back to the bed by the light of the last oil lamp and prayed not to have any dreams.

4

Why does she smell like tears?
        Did I hurt her?

I stayed on the couch when she returned, like I was already asleep. We both knew it was untrue, but I didn't think she'd test me again tonight.

I wanted to ask her so many things. Where was Vincent? Had he ever mentioned me? Did she know who I was to him – what we'd had? Did anyone?

For the past seven years I felt like I'd been carrying memories for the both of us. I was glad to have them, but Christ they were heavy. I knew I couldn't be with him anymore, and I knew why – but I wanted to know that I wasn't the only one it hurt.

I heard her breathing even out as she truly fell asleep, and I allowed myself to doze.

"WE DID IT, MAX –" Vincent looked over at me with a positively wolfish grin. We were in some metal and cement pit by the ports and there were three bodies between us, plus one more outside. "They didn't hear us coming."

Well, they had, but the one who was supposed to warn them I'd killed quickly. The darkness gave me enough cover to act faster than any human could, slapping his gun away before breaking his neck. Vincent hadn't seen me and conveniently the dead guy couldn't testify.

"Want me to clean this up?" I asked, toeing the nearest corpse.

"No. Leave them here. The Carminos will find out before the cops." He closed a briefcase that I was very sure was full of hundred dollar bills. "They'll get the message."

"Which is?"

He tucked the briefcase under one arm. "The docks are ours."

I opened my mouth to ask more, then closed it again. I knew from watching TV and reading news that getting involved in mob business was a bad idea. Watching Vincent get involved was bad enough – only where he was concerned, I couldn't help myself. My wolf and I needed an alpha, and we'd both latched on to him.

He crossed the room, still smiling, warming me like the sun as he neared. "Don't look like that, Max. We're gonna go celebrate. Come on. Let me show you a good time."

He turned and I followed, obediently.

CELEBRATIONS FOR VINCENT involved a lot of booze with a light dusting of cocaine. I'd lived with him for three months, long enough to know he'd never become an addict – he enjoyed living his own life too much for that. But what was the point of being young and thus far invincible if you couldn't push your nights out hard?

We went for the booze first, pressing into local bars and getting treated like a regular, even where we weren't. He clapped backs and shouted greetings, me always one step behind him, eyes and ears alert. News of our success preceded us or Vincent shared it along the way. People were happy for him, he was an *up-and-comer*, one to *keep-*

an-eye-on, had *beginner's-luck*, or was a *smug-asshole*, depending on who I overheard.

I watched their faces as Vincent became more inebriated, coming in and out of bathrooms with a powdered nose. While half of them were genuinely happy for him, the other half smiled with just their eyes, their mouths giving way to jealousy. I made sure to stand close – I knew from my time as a fighter that the only thing more enjoyable than watching someone charismatic succeed was watching their subsequent downfall.

"Drink some," Vincent begged, by the third bar. He was swaying a little, eyes bright.

I shook my head. I had to stay straight, for his sake. "Maybe back at the condo, Sir," I said.

"Vincent," he corrected, like I didn't know his name. Two men he knew approached him with exclamations and clapping hugs, and one of them mentioned his cousin's strip club. A minute after that I was fetching the car.

THE CLUB WAS JUST ABOUT to close when we got there, but between the relative's connection, the men's suits, and Vincent's bankroll, the club stayed open just for the three of them.

Soon Vincent and his friends each had a half-dressed woman on their lap, with others lounging seductively nearby. Unfortunately they hadn't sent the DJ home yet either, so the bass of the club was unrelenting, each thump making my listening wolf whine in pain.

"Not even now?" Vincent asked, lolling his head back, trying to shove a blonde woman at me.

Chemicals, my wolf hissed. The scent of sweat and arousal in here was good – the scent of cherry body lotion was not. "No, thank you," I said, gently pushing her back to the throng.

"Your loss," Vincent said, as one of the others took the stage to perform.

Everyone was quiet, watching her rhythmic dancing. She was the kind of woman sometimes I'd luck into after a fight, one so turned on by the spectacle that she'd forget where she was or that I was poor – and the way she moved, my wolf could overlook the cherries. Three months was a tortuously long time to be celibate – especially when you were living with a man you wanted to fuck.

"See what you're missing?" Vincent asked, looking back up at me. I flushed, and he laughed. "Come on ladies – it's time for us to go home."

Vincent's announcement was met with *Awwwww*'s, and, *don't go yet!*'s but he ignored them and looked at me. "Get the car."

I surveyed the room one last time for safety's sake, then left to do as I was told.

THE VALET they had let go. I grabbed our keyring and went out into the streets, canvassing until I found where he'd parked our car earlier, and came back. When I got back into the club, most of the girls were gone, and so was he.

"Where's V?" I asked the blonde with a big bag tucked under her arm.

"He's taking a piss," she said, checking her make-up out in a compact mirror. She was clothed now, in a blue-sequined dress, and between that and her long blonde hair she looked like half a mermaid.

The brunette who'd been on Vincent's lap was off talking to a guy – the owner of the club? – whose eyes narrowed when he looked at me. The music hadn't stopped yet, so I couldn't hear what they were saying.

Vincent emerged from the bathroom and swooped forward, putting an arm around the blonde. The brunette trotted over on impossible heels to catch up – my wolf saw *broken ankles* and *easy kill!* and I had to push it down to make it shut up – until she took her place on Vincent's other side.

"Follow this man, ladies – he'll never lead you astray," Vincent said, stumbling forward while pointing at me. I held the doors of the club open for all of them, then helped them into the backseat of the waiting car.

I PRETENDED NOT to notice or care what they did on the way to the condo, even though there was no way not to hear the sound of their kisses, their moans, and smell the scents of their arousal. My heart beat low inside my chest, my wolf jealous, wanting the feel of skin, any skin.

I let all of them out of the backseat and herded them toward the elevator. Vincent gave me a look over their heads as they lounged on him, groping at his chest, kissing his neck, all of them leaning against the wall.

"You sure?" he asked me, mouthing the words.

I nodded and looked away, until the elevator found our floor.

He unlocked the condo and went with them into his bedroom. I sat on the couch, listening.

It wasn't the first night I'd spent like this, and it wouldn't be the last. Why was I here? Why did I torment myself like this? The money was good, but I didn't need money, I knew how to get by without it. I could always fight again if I had to, or just live off the land as a wolf – a full wolf's belly was just as good as a full human one.

The door unlocked, and Vincent emerged. He was naked from the waist up, and I could see lipstick marks on his neck like bloody bites as he walked over to the bar.

"Are you completely sure you don't want one of them?"

I shook my head. "I'm fine."

He sighed and contemplated me, drink in hand. "You've got to learn how to celebrate more, Max. How to lose control every once in a while. Otherwise everything's going to build up in you and someday you'll explode."

He set his drink down and began making two more. "You could take one to your own room, you know. If that's what's holding you back," he said, as I stood to help him carry the other drinks. He smelled so good, the scent I'd become accustomed to while living with him, his musk and a hint of his aftershave. The stripper was right to have kissed his neck, if our situations were reversed I would have started there too and then gone lower, fast –

Vincent looked at me as though I'd been considering his offer. I quickly shook my head again. "Not tonight. Thank you."

"Your loss, Max," he said, his voice quiet, putting his drink inside the bedroom, and then taking the other two from me quickly, and closing the door.

I went back to my vigil on the couch, listening to them fuck, trying to ignore my erection.

Twenty minutes later I stood up. I was going to go take a shower and jerk off with the remnants of my dignity – that way I'd be done and dry before the strippers needed rides.

The bathroom smelled like him, which didn't help. His shaving cream, his cologne. I pulled my shirt off and put it beside the sink. In the mirror I could see down to my hips. So many scars I'd gotten, fighting other weres. A full set of wolf-teeth marked my arm, and five gouges streaked across my stomach, where Syd had been half a pound of pressure away from disemboweling me.

Other weres hadn't come of age and sometimes looked for dicks to suck. What I was was an aberration – no matter how many of the older pack members had furtively fucked me, before I was kicked out. I had to abide by their rules still – but none of them could stand to be around me.

Which left me to take care of myself. Like always. I rested one hand on the belt of my pants and was reaching the other one down to cup my balls when I heard the distinctive sound of a gun being unholstered in the condo's hallway outside. I had one second to dive to the ground before they shot the handle off the front door.

THE WOMEN SCREAMED and I prayed that the alcohol had made Vincent slow, as one of the men outside walked in. I waited until the last moment before rushing into the living room and throwing myself against the loose door on him with wolf-strength. He dropped instantly with a concussion and a bleeding broken nose – and the next man in the hall shouted in surprise. I took a risk and leapt for him, getting too close too fast for him to use the gun, and reached for his throat, breaking his windpipe with one hand. A second later Vincent was in the hall, naked, except for a Steyr TMP.

"What the hell?" he said, surveying the situation, gun ready.

"Grab the girls' phones – someone told these idiots you were home and occupied." I bent over to grab one ankle of each man and dragged both of them into the condo.

Vincent left to do as I said and I heard screams of protest from the other room. He returned with pants on, hauling the brunette out.

"Who'd you tell?" he said, holding her phone.

"I can't tell you –" she said, squirming in his arms. She looked even more like prey in that moment, her eyes wild. My wolf salivated, wanting to see her try to *run.*

"You do realize that those men were going to kill you, too, don't you?" I told her. As the only sober person in the room, my voice had some authority. "Whoever planned this wasn't going to leave witnesses."

She shook her head and her eyes went even wider. Vincent hugged her close. "Tell me who planned it and I let you go. Don't, and I keep you here overnight, and say you tipped me off."

I looked over to him as she gasped. Even intoxicated, my alpha was in control.

"It was Jimmy – but you can't tell him I told you –" she turned in his arms, from escaping to clinging. "You have to give me some money, help me to run."

Vincent shrugged, cold. "You don't deserve anything, after selling me out. Go –" he pointed towards the broken door.

"But –" she whined.

"If you talk to me again I'll have Max kill you."

She looked over at me – and at the bodies on the floor, downed by my hand. *That's right. I'm the the big bad wolf.* Furiously pissed but more frightened, she took off with just the clothing on her back.

Vincent watched her go then turned to me. "Give the other girl a couple of hundred, and get her out. I need to make some calls."

I got the money out of Vincent's petty cash drawer and rousted the blonde, who was too high or drunk to care. By the time I'd gotten her to the elevator and back, Vincent was done.

I knew he had bosses who had bosses, and he himself had men beneath him, other soldiers – they gave me curt nods when our paths overlapped. What I didn't know was that there was a cavalry for situations just like this – within thirty minutes, our penthouse was like an Amish barn raising of forensic disposal. People showed up to change the door, clean the floor, take the one body away, the other man in to interrogate, and threaten or bribe neighbors on other floors into silence. Thirty minutes after that, Vincent and I were alone again.

He was sober now and I noticed he hadn't shared the information the brunette had given him with the boss or the workerbees that'd shown up. I knew from living with him that his revenge would be personal – and hoped I'd be lucky enough to get involved in it.

He was sitting on his couch much as I had earlier, elbows on knees, his head in his hands.

I went to the bar and made him a drink, the last of his whiskey and two ice cubes, the way I knew he liked it. "You'll have to move now."

"I know," he said, taking the drink from my hand.

It wasn't that where he lived was a secret, but there were too many neighbors here – and not enough brick to catch stray bullets.

"This is not how I thought things were going to go. Tonight was going to be my night." He rocked back into the couch and looked up at me, giving me a sly smile without taking a sip of his drink.

"I'm sorry your celebrations were interrupted."

He shrugged one shoulder, still eyeing me. "They hadn't really started yet."

It was times like these that made working for him worthwhile – when my wolf's tail beat in hope – until I caught myself and realized that I was just projecting, and reality dashed me against the rocks.

"You knew there'd be trouble tonight. And –" he hoisted his drink up in a kind of a toast. "You know me better than I know myself."

"Sir," I said, looking away.

"Vincent," he corrected softly. "You're so obedient, Max. Sometimes I get the idea I could ask you to do anything."

My stomach tensed and my chest started to rise. If there was ever a time to be brave, to tell him the truth about me, this was it.

"You could, if you wanted to," I said, without daring to look up.

He made a thoughtful sound and I waited. For him to throw me out, for him to yell, for him to laugh it off, brush it under the rug and blame too much to drink.

When he didn't I let my gaze rise, from his feet to his chest to his face, where he was watching me with his dark eyes. He slid one hand to rest between his open legs.

"Come here and suck my cock, Max."

I fell to all fours and crawled over to him, to do as I was told – and by the time I'd gotten there, his dick was free, pulled over by its weight to arch between the flat plane of his stomach and his thigh.

I didn't dare use a hand, I just leaned in and licked up, from the edge of his balls up his shaft. He tasted like salt and sweat and the wolf in me wanted to rub my face against him, to take his scent with me when this was through – I caught the thick head of his cock in my lips and started working my way down.

"That's good," he said, sliding a hand into my hair and pulling it with just the right amount of tension. "You've done this before. I can tell. No hesitation." He pulled my mouth off of him, making his heavy cock bump against my chin before it dropped. I licked my lips hoping for more as his hand let go. "Not trying to use me."

I swallowed. "The opposite, in fact," I confessed.

His mouth curved into a wicked smile. "Pull yourself out, Max. And stroke yourself while you suck me."

His words sent reverberations through my core, and my hands went to do as they were told before I was capable of conscious thought. I was hard, *fuck, so hard* already, my dick was just waiting to spring out. I took him up in one hand, bringing his head to my lips again, as I started stroking myself, doing exactly what I was told.

His hand went back into my hair, but he didn't force himself into me – I felt like he wanted to see what I would do – like I was auditioning. I stroked my tongue up him and ran it against the edge of his opening, and the gasp he gave somehow made me harder still.

I sucked him down, feeling him bend as he hit the back of my throat, rolling my lips up and down him, again and again, pulling at him, letting him know how much I wanted him inside. He tasted so good and the noises he made turned me on – my own cock was rock hard as I stroked it the way I liked, fast and light, and if he didn't come soon I was going to have to pinch my tip to stop myself.

Vincent's hand shifted in my hair, like he was trying to hold on, grunting, so close to losing control. "Come like you're going to make me come, Max," he demanded. "Spill it on my floor so I can fucking come in you."

That growl, that tone, that confidence – my wolf recognized it, and *needed* it, the same as I did. I rose up on my knees, my face buried in Vincent's lap, my screaming muffled as I came, jerking to completion as he used my mouth for its final sucks. The taste of him burst across my tongue and I lapped it up, swallowing.

I pulled myself off of him, and he looked down at me from above. Divinely in control, everything I needed. *Alpha,* my wolf whined, and I agreed.

After that, all of his celebrating took place in private – with me.

I woke to discover the prior night had not been a dream – I had indeed come home with a strange woman – and we had fucked, I could still smell it in the air. More than that, I could smell *him*.

No wonder I'd dreamed of him last night. My erection was still straining. *God. Even after all this time.* I stood up quietly, walking over to her. She smelled so like him – I leaned over and breathed her in, the scent making my heart and balls ache. I quickly went outside, locking the door behind me.

I leaned against one of the timbers supporting the porch. I'd been living like a hermit, and now, after last night – it was like a genie'd been released. My wolf rose up in me with *needs* – there was no way I could hunt like this, not when I wanted to fuck so badly. I opened up my jeans and pushed them down to reach for myself, imagining it was Vincent's hand, not mine, stroking me. The way he'd reach down during sex, to finish me off, the nights with his hands, his mouth, his tongue – I gasped, shooting my load out, taking a step forward, falling into the past, for a man who wasn't there. I sagged against the timber and collected myself. I just – had to keep her safe – I just – needed to *run* and *hunt*.

I stumbled towards the treeline, and the freedom of four legs.

5

I sat up in bed when I heard the door close and it all came rushing back. I was here in Redneckania alone – for real, because Max wasn't on the couch. Maybe he had to pee or something. *Or go out to get us bagels.* I sighed.

How long could I keep this up, not telling him what'd happened? Another day or two at most. He had a truck, he could go into town, Vincent's death would have made the newspaper at least. Just because he lived in the middle of nowhere didn't mean he was dumb.

And then what? I leaned over the bed and looked to where I'd stashed my bag underneath. Maybe a few days were all I needed to get away safely. Ask him to drive me to an airport, bribe him with a bundle of twenties or a blowjob. I curled up on the uncomfortable mattress, knees under my chin.

I saw a movement out of the corner of my eye, through one of the windows. I crawled over carefully and peered out. He was outside. Just standing there, leaning – *oh ho ho.*

Taking care of himself. I recognized the hand movements.

I bet he had to do that a lot out here. Probably fucked the holes of trees for fun. I watched him shamelessly, getting to see what I hadn't last night, the length and girth of him as he worked himself over. Last night had been good...on the scale of things to distract me from my newly dead boyfriend. I closed my eyes and put my head against the windowpane. The next time I opened them, he was gone.

Good. I stood up and stretched, and went for the front door. I'd walk around outside some, get back into touch with nature, pretend I was at some sort of spa. I grabbed the handle and turned – and it wouldn't give. What?

"Hey – hey!" I rattled it back and forth in its frame. The bastard had locked me in. "Hey!" I slammed a fist into my side of the door. Why did he do that? Was he already selling me out?

"Let me the fuck out of here!" I shouted. No one came in response.

I SPENT what felt like an eternity with my legs crossed. When he came back, I shoved my way out the door and ran to the outhouse – and when I came back, I made sure to stand on the porch and not go inside.

"Where were you? I had to pee so bad I almost died."

"I left you a bucket," he said, pointing to one side.

"Are you kidding me?" His expression said that he was not. "Why the hell did you lock me in?"

"To protect you."

"From what?"

"Bears. Mountain lions."

His face was so serious, I was inclined to believe him, even though I was still royally pissed off.

"No tigers?" I suggested, sarcastically. His eyebrows rose. "You know? From the Wizard of Oz? Lions and tigers and bears, oh my?"

He shook his head. "No. This is dangerous country."

I crossed my arms, unwilling to forgive him. "So where were you?"

"Hunting."

I looked at him. "With just...you? No gun, no bow and arrows?"

He shrugged. "Yeah."

"Did it work?"

"No," he said, shrugging again.

I calmed down slowly. If he'd sold me out, the Carminos would have been here already, three hours was more than enough time. I didn't believe anything else about him further than I could throw him, though.

"Is there someplace in this godforsaken forest that I can take a bath?" I felt dirty after last night – I wanted to wash everything away.

"There's a creek. I can take you there."

"Good."

I followed him down the ridge in my robe and shoes. Even though it was almost noon, birds were still chirping overhead, and squirrels were jumping from branch to branch. Fat rabbits raced away in the underbrush, and we startled a deer with a fawn, pausing to watch them both leap away. All this exuberant 'nature' made me feel like a low rent Snow White.

The cabin was over a creek, if you walked far enough out in a straight line. And some person had dammed a portion of it, creating a little watering hole that was lined with rushes on one side. I stood at the edge of this, my hand on my robe's tie, and looked to him.

Despite last night he turned around so he wouldn't see me. I appreciated that. I carefully set my robe down and walked to the water's edge, gasping as it touched my toes.

"What?" he said, turning fast.

"It's cold," I protested, arms crossed over my breasts. The locket swung between them, the only thing I wore.

"Sorry," he said, and returned to steadfastly looking away from me.

I grit my teeth and slowly walked in, waist deep, my feet slipping over rocks on the bottom, worried about snapping turtles biting off my toes.

How did those old timey baptisms work? You dove underneath the water a sinner, and afterwards came up clean? I held my breath and tried it. It didn't feel like it'd changed anything.

I untangled my wet hair with one hand, body mostly hidden by the water. With the sound of the cicadas and the rippling of the creek – everything was peaceful out here, except for me. I looked up at him, still angled away. "How did you know Vincent?"

He was silent for so long I thought maybe he hadn't heard me. "It's hard to explain," he said at long last.

For seven years, I'd known Vincent inside and out, and I'd never once heard him mention knowing a mountain man. He had to have been one of Vincent's old employees, back from when he ran fights, someone who'd then decided to go native.

But why? Who was he hiding from out here? Who'd hurt him this badly? His fingers pulled three pieces of grass up and I watched him braid them rather than talk to me.

"You haven't even asked me what my name is."

"What's your name?" he asked, without looking up.

"Sarah," I lied.

"Nice to meet you, Sarah."

"Nice to meet you, too, Max," I muttered under my breath, and dipped under the water again.

HE FOLLOWED me back to the cabin – to see if I'd find my way back, I thought – and then we stood at an impasse on the porch.

"I don't have dinner yet – you need to go inside."

"Why?"

"Because I have to go out hunting again."

"With your bare hands. Like a ninja." He glowered at me. It might have worked on other women, but I was used to Vincent so I held my ground.

"I set traps earlier. It's not humane to leave animals in them – plus if I don't collect them, other predators will."

My eyes narrowed at him including himself among their number. *Lions and tigers and Maxes, oh my.* "You can't lock me in again."

"You don't understand –"

"I may not," I interrupted. "But I don't want to be trapped." He didn't look like he would break, but I wanted to see how far I could push him. "What if there's a fire?"

His strong jaw clenched as he held words back. "Stay on the porch then. But don't go walking around. I can't protect you out there." He gestured behind himself, and I got the feeling he meant all of the civilization past the trees too.

"Okay," I promised.

He sighed deeply, giving me a distrustful look, but then turned and stalked back into the woods.

I watched him go more closely than I should have. He was handsome underneath his gruff exterior. He walked the land like he was born to it, with competence that made him instantly attractive, and I knew that underneath his shirt and jeans he'd be lean and muscled. If he really did live off the land up here, he probably didn't have an ounce of body fat on him.

Vincent would've liked him. My man sometimes had things for other men.

"I just don't want to scare you off," he said, smiling down at me.

We'd moved in together, in a way – he'd bought me a hotel room to live in, and he had the only other key. It wasn't quite like being Suzie Homemaker, but it was close enough for a whore.

"All right," I said, reluctantly. I was in a short black dress and tied to a chair, my legs spread wide, ankles lashed to chair legs, with my arms behind my back, making my chest jut forward. I knew I was beautiful like this, in that way only he and I could appreciate.

"Only two things left. Three, really." He knelt down, and I could feel his heat and smell him as he leaned over me, putting something small and round into my hand. "If you want this to end, you just drop that, okay?"

"Okay," I nodded. "But why can't I –"

Vincent held up a small ball-gag, before I could ask. He proffered it out to me, like asking a horse to take the bit of a bridle. We'd done this before. I opened my mouth and let him place it inside.

"Last, but not least, this – just for now," he promised, and tugged a blindfold down, so all I could see was black.

We'd played these games before, but something about Vincent now was strange – he was nervous. He was never nervous around me – I did whatever he said, there was no need. I tensed in the chair, suddenly feeling trapped.

Then there was a knock at the door.

"Hey," Vincent answered as the door opened.

"Hey," said someone else's voice. "Wow – she's beautiful."

"Uh-huh," Vincent agreed.

I swallowed, as my heart began to race. He'd brought someone else in here. Who were they? Was he going to share me with them?

I heard the unfamiliar voice chuckle, and then the groaning of the bedsprings as they both sat down on the bed. I tensed, on tip-toes, leaning forward as much as my tied arms would let me – then heard the soft wet sound of shared kisses, and Vincent, I knew it was him, catch his breath.

My mouth fell open around the gag as I listened to them disrobe. The rustle of fabrics, as buttons were undone and flies unzipped. Together their breathing picked up, low and rough, and I could easily imagine where their hands were going, what they were doing to one another, laying side by side. Then I heard a sharp intake of breath, and another of Vincent's groans, more guttural – and I knew the stranger's mouth was on his cock. Vincent moaned again, and the other man grunted, and I knew my man was giving his cock to him, fucking his mouth and throat.

I felt a pang at that – sucking him was my job, and I didn't want to share. I shook my head, trying to dislodge the blindfold, willing it down, jealous – and hungry. There was no way not to imagine them while I listened to their sounds, and I could almost smell the sex. The ropes around me chafed but not as much as being on the sidelines did.

When I heard the familiar sound of a condom wrapper being opened I gave in, and dropped the ball I was holding.

The action on the bed stopped, and I felt a presence in front of me. Vincent tugged the blindfold down. He was naked and beautiful, scars, tattoo, and an erection.

"Are you okay?" he asked.

I looked over his shoulder. There was another man on the bed too, one a little younger than Vincent was, with more of a dancer's build, not a fighter, but he was every bit as undressed. I still had the gag in, so I couldn't answer Vincent, but I prayed he would see it in my eyes.

He gave me a pensive look – and reached between my legs. I gasped in surprise, and his expression went from worried to pleased with what he found there.

"Do you want to watch?" he asked, massaging my panties into the wetness of my pussy. I nodded. "Or do you want to play?" he asked. I nodded twice as hard.

"All right then," he said with a satisfied grin. He knelt to untie my legs and arms. When I reached for the gag's ties, he pushed my hands down. "Your mouth is just for me. Take your clothes off."

I hurried to do as I was told, and when I was as naked as they were he smiled, taking one of my hands to pull me to the bed like I was an arriving queen. The other man looked up at me appraisingly, while playing with his cock. "Sammy, meet Angel. Angel, meet Sammy." Vincent spun me and pushed me on my ass into the bed. "I'm going to be fucking the shit out of both of you tonight."

And I learned that while you may not be able to talk around a ball-gag, you can definitely scream around one.

I SAT on the porch and touched myself beneath my robe. Just like Max had earlier in the day, I couldn't help it. If I kept my eyes closed, I could remember Vincent's hands stroking me, what it'd felt like to be pinned by his cock, see his face with each thrust, hear the sounds of pleasure he made when he came in me. There were nights when he wouldn't come at all, when he'd just torture me, bringing me close with his fingers and tongue and then falling away like the tide to other parts, sucking my nipples, kissing the backs of my knees, until it'd seemed like my chance to come was lost, and then he'd push his fingers back inside me – like I was pushing mine now, trying to recreate something now forever lost – "Vincent," I whispered to myself, rocking on the wood, pretending that the sun beaming down was his heat on me. My hips felt full, I needed it, *I needed it*, **I needed it** – my orgasm gasped out of me as I rocked on the wood, quiet waves crashing on a smooth stoned beach. I sat there, panting, my hand slicked with my wetness, and sagged against the nearest timber.

Coming seemed to have granted me some clarity. I had to get it together. I had to come up with a plan for the future. A timeline. I stood and took a deep breath. No matter what I'd promised Mountain Max, I needed to pace to think, and I couldn't do that inside.

Since whatever way he took into the forest was probably safest, I followed his path in.

It wasn't as scary as I'd thought it'd be. What I was on wasn't precisely a path but I knew where the cabin was and I wasn't planning on making sudden turns. Branches and bark caught at my robe, so I tucked it up around me, ever so glad I'd packed appropriate footwear back in the day.

When had Vincent known it'd been too late and decommissioned his own go-bag? I tried to think back, worried that I'd missed signs. He'd been more stressed than usual – and a few months ago Syd had come over, and Vincent had made me go away and wouldn't tell me what they'd talked about afterwards –

Lost in my own thoughts, I missed a stick jutting out from a fallen branch. It scraped across my ankle, drawing blood. "Shit –" I knelt down. I doubted Max had any Neosporin up here. I licked my thumb and rubbed the blood away – and saw what looked like...jeans.

I took another step forward. They *were* jeans – and a shirt. The same ones I'd seen Max wear out the door. His boots, too.

What the hell?

I stood and looked around. Was he...out here? Naked? Doing... what? Watching me? The rustling branches of trees that'd seemed so calming before now sounded ominous. I turned and ran until I reached the cabin's porch.

6

I trotted through the forest, carrying a rabbit in my jaws. I was hungry and wanted all of it, *blood and bone*, but remembered that I needed to share, so I only gnawed its head off, to share the rest with *mate-smell* person. I shook my head at my wolf's foolishness, making the rabbit bob. Just because Sarah smelled like Vincent did not mean she was a mate. That was just crazy.

I stopped in a hole I'd dug into the side of a hill, and pulled my wolf back in, feeling the *pop and stretch* of realigning skin and bones, until found myself gasping in the dirt, naked. The change always hurt, even when you were prepared for it.

I could only protect her for three more days before I needed to figure out somewhere else for her to go – or for Vincent to come and get her back. I was my wolf's master for now, but when the moon was full – Vincent had to know that when he'd sent her to me. He remembered, I was sure of it. I stumbled out of the hole like I'd just been born, blinking in the daylight, and picked the rabbit's carcass up to walk back to where I'd left my clothes earlier.

Two steps away from the clearing, I paused.

Something smelled like her.

Was it my clothing? Because she'd spent the night? No – it was stronger. I crouched down, feeling foolish on all fours as a human – but my wolf found the fresh scent of *blood*.

She'd been here. Like I'd told her not to. Shit. *How would I explain this?* I wondered, tugging my pants on. Did I have to? Did I owe her an explanation? Not really. I was doing her a favor – doing Vincent a favor, not even her. I hauled my shirt on and buttoned it and stalked back to the cabin, expecting to find her standing outside, mouth full of questions. When she wasn't there I took the stairs and stopped, halfway up, scenting something unusual and yet familiar. *Sex*, my wolf informed me with a whine.

My hand on the rabbit's legs clenched. What was she thinking? You couldn't just go leaving all sorts of smells out here. It wasn't safe. This was pack land.

I WALKED INTO THE CABIN, braced for questions. Instead she just looked up at me from the couch, where she was thumbing through what might've been the oldest copy of National Geographic in the world.

"You're back," she said, with a sexy voice.

I nodded, and held the rabbit up. "See?"

She blanched. I'd eaten its head off as a wolf, but the rest of it was intact and bloody.

"I'll be back," I said, excusing myself, taking a knife and going back outside to clean the meat.

In a few moments, she was at my side. *Here it'd come.*

"Is there anything I can do to help?"

I looked over at her, one hand full of rabbit guts. "Not really."

She made a face – not at what I was doing, but at being rebuffed. "I don't like feeling useless."

I stopped my knife from raking a familiar path down the rabbit's spine, and thought hard. "You can stoke the fire. And find a can of beans in the pantry – don't worry about the expiration dates. And when we're done eating, you can take the dishes down to the creek and wash them."

"Okay." She nodded, sending a dirty-blonde wave of hair bobbing over one eye. *Sarah-good-smell-sex*, my wolf muttered.

I swallowed, and I didn't dare to look over at her again as she went inside.

WITHIN AN HOUR she was scraping meat with her teeth off of rabbit bones. "This is pretty good."

"Yeah," I agreed. I did most of my eating as a wolf, because what was the point of cooking without company?

It'd been so long I'd forgotten all the problems that having company could bring. Like conversations – and questions. There was no way she hadn't seen my clothes out there today – but if she wasn't going to ask, I wasn't going to offer answers.

She set the bones down on her plate, and came over with it to reach for mine. As she leaned over I could feel-smell the heat of her, the blood at her throat, the fatty weight of her breasts.

"I'll be right back," she promised.

I quickly glanced out a window. "Don't bother. It's almost dark."

"It's not that far –" she protested, still hovering.

"I'll take you there tomorrow and make sure you know the path." I took the plate from her hand and roughly set it down.

It was time to talk. I couldn't keep waiting for her to tell me things about him, I'd have to ask questions, even if asking made me weak – even if she told me answers I didn't want to know. I grabbed her hand before she could pull away. "Sarah – where is he?"

Her face clouded – and at the same time I heard a distant howl.

"Fuck." I turned towards the window. The howl dropped and then restarted. I knew who it was – Karl, Syd's errand-boy – and where he was. I stood, pushing her back. "I've got to go."

"What – why?"

"No time to explain." I started for the door, and then turned. She'd come after me once before – I couldn't take that chance again. Not with pack outside. I picked her up and threw her bodily onto the mattress.

"What're you doing?" she shouted.

I planted a hand over her face and hissed, "Shut up." I grabbed hold of a pillowcase and flung the pillow out of it, then gagged her with it while her hands scrabbled at me, leaving long gashes with her nails. I could scent her terror, the bile rising in her throat, as I wound the rest of the sheets around her, hands and ankles, tying her to the bedframe. Her eyes were wild and she was afraid of me, truly afraid. I breathed over her, for a moment feeling like the monster she thought I was.

The howl called again. If I didn't answer quickly, Karl would come for me.

"I'll be back," I told her, realizing that might not be particularly comforting.

I stripped off my clothing the second I made it into the woods, and hurled myself down into my wolf's form, feeling the *pop and change*, a fraction of a second before I hit the ground. Rebounding on all fours, I howled back to Karl, a warning, *this is my land, come no further*, although both of us knew the truth. My job was to discourage humans from coming onto pack land, and to keep it free of traps, but I was only left alone out here because Syd didn't consider me a threat.

The only time I'd gotten to be in peace in my own skin, or as a wolf, had been with *him*.

BLOWJOBS, morning, noon, and night. That was how it'd started. I craved to serve him. Any time I could take his cock into my mouth I would. Kneeling in front of him, eyes closed, feeling him slide in and out of me, hearing his grunts and gasps as I sucked on him until he came, him looking down the flat washboard of his stomach at me, jaw dropped in disbelief. I licked all of him, wanting to taste all his skin, leaving nothing hidden. The scent of his musk, the dewy drops of his precum, the feel of his hands on my back as he bent over to moan. I worshipped him like a beast designed for it, trading my pleasures for his, knowing that I would satisfy him and through that, satisfy myself.

We didn't leave his new house for three days, because I needed him and he wanted me.

His hands flowed over my back and chest, fingers raking through my hair, but anytime he ever reached for my cock, I pushed his hands away. But this time I reached for him, he pushed *me* back, bodily. He rose up on his elbows on his old bed in his new bedroom and stared at me as I looked up at him in confusion.

"Max – don't you ever want more?"

I froze. I knew from long experience that packmembers who asked for too much got beaten down, so I didn't dare say a word, no matter how much the wolf inside me whined. His eyes traced over my body, looking at my chest, my stomach, my scars, then met my gaze again.

"I want more. Even if you don't," he said.

I swallowed, tense, hoping.

"Come here, Max. Obey," he said, trying out the words as if for the first time.

I crawled up the bed to be beside him. I still had my jeans on, I hadn't wanted him to see how hard sucking on him made me.

He rose up beside me, pushing me down. He was breathing hard, turned on by the power of taking control over me – as turned on as I was to relinquish it. He wanted to be an alpha, and I yearned to have one care for me.

He leaned over and rubbed me through my jeans. "I want to fuck you, Max. Not just your mouth – your ass."

If I currently had a tail, it would've dropped. I'd never let a human mount me before. I'd only taken desperate fuckings from other weres who would pretend not to know me five seconds after they came.

"You can't –" I said, biting back all the rules and reasons.

"I don't care," he said, looking down at me with a cruel smile. "You like me when I'm willful and arrogant. You like being needed – being used." He leaned over me, chest to chest, his hand still hot over my cock. "I need to fuck you Max. I want to use your ass."

I made a strangled sound, and inside me my wolf crouched and whined. We both wanted this. I started panting as he undid the top button of my jeans, yanking them down, exposing my swollen cock. He bent over then to kiss me as I'd so often kissed him, sucking my head with his soft lips as his fingers stroked my shaft.

"Vincent –" I gasped.

"Yes," he said, not in response, but in triumph.

I squirmed out of the rest of my jeans without thinking. It was now now now – I turned over, presenting myself to be taken, ready to feel him inside of me.

"No," he chided, pushing me down and rolling me back, exposing my belly, my cock swinging across it like a pendulum. "Like this," he said, moving to kneel in front of me.

"Why?" Weres didn't fuck like that, was this a human thing?

He smiled at me softly. "So I can see your face when I'm fucking you," he explained, his voice low, as he slid himself in.

He fucked me more slowly than weres fucked. Weres were all dominance and violence and getting themselves off. If Syd ever knew how many of his pack had broken rank to roughly fuck me, he would have never let me leave alive.

But Vincent was thorough, and as his hard cock slid in and out of my ass, he reached for my cock and stroked its shaft and I moaned. I brought a hand up to take my cock from him and he stopped thrusting.

"Stop," he commanded, and I set my hand down, staring up. "You're mine. All mine," he said, stroking me as he took another thrust.

It'd never been like this before at all. Ever. No one had ever told me to just relax, to just let myself be fucked. It was hard to go with the moment until he started taking my ass in earnest, while still holding on to my cock. I whined and he grunted as the tension between us grew, the friction of his cock inside me and his hand fucking my dick – I felt my balls begin to lift and knew I was almost past the point where I could stop – all I knew anymore was that I didn't want him too – my ass clenched around him tight, as tight as his hand pulled on me, and he fucked me hard as he gasped, shooting his load deep inside me while mine spilled out all over his hand.

He leaned over me, holding himself up with his clean hand, looking down at my sweaty face. No were had ever wanted to see my face while fucking before – nor had they wanted me to see theirs.

And then he grinned, mischievous, and painted a mark on my chest with my cum as though he'd claimed me. I knew then, even though he had no mating knot to tie me with, I was chained.

That night I slept outside his room, guarding his closed door.

I RACED through the forest on all fours, feeling the power surge through me, baited on by the waxing moon overhead, until I found myself in a clearing with a naked man.

I concentrated. The fur twisted in, man-skin spread out, and we were both naked.

Karl looked at me appraisingly. "Living rough's been good to you, Max."

He was as tall as I was, but doughy and pale. There was gray around his hairline now that hadn't been there when I'd last seen his human form, years ago. "City life's making you fat. Why're you here Karl? Other than to check up on me?"

He gave me a smug look. "Thought you'd like to know your old employer's died."

I didn't say anything at first. Karl was an asshole, and I wouldn't put it past him to come up here just to try to get a rise out of me. But then I saw the gleam in his eye, him preparing for joy from causing me pain. "What? How –"

Karl looked at me like I was daft. "Come on, you knew his line of work."

"But –" I felt as though I'd been punched in the chest by a giant and the world was swinging round.

"We're still looking for his bitch – she was going to turn evidence in. She got him killed."

I tried, and failed, to get control. I thought I might throw up.

"Did you know of any hideouts he had? Places she might have known about to go hole up?" he pressed.

I somehow managed not to sway. "I haven't seen him or spoken to him in seven years."

"I know. But you two were friends. Better than friends," he said, with that same smug expression. "I remember seeing you two –"

I stared at him with dead eyes. "That's enough." My voice was like a whip crack in the night, we both could hear it echo.

Karl leered, unstoppable. "How long's it been since you got fucked out here, Maxie? You still like it rough?"

"Shut up, Karl."

He reached for his crotch. "How about a suck for old times sake? You used to love my cock."

Hackles on my wolf's neck rose. "I'm different now."

"My wolf could order you to do it."

"But right now I'm a man," I said, flexing my muscles just enough to be a threat, not a challenge.

He snorted. "Whatever, I have pussy at home to fuck. You think of anything, you let me know though." He rolled his shoulders, and descended back to the road.

I stood there until I heard the sound of his car drive off.

Vincent...was dead?

My leaving him was supposed to buy him safety. I needed these last seven, awful, torturous years, trapped in the mountains, alone, to not have been in vain.

And yet now he was gone.

It was one thing knowing he was alive somewhere without me – that was bad enough. But at least he'd been alive. There'd been hope, somehow, me seeing his smile, me catching his scent. How many times had I gone into town for supplies and prayed to a God I didn't believe in for His mercy, that I might catch an improbable glance of him at the discount food store?

All I wanted was for there to be an *us* again.

But now...there was only death and ash.

Waves of anger and grief rolled through me, wracking through my soul. So many things I hadn't gotten to tell him, so many things we hadn't done. My true alpha, gone.

Why didn't she tell me?

I stumbled through the trees as a human, feeling the branches rake and tear, stones cutting the bottoms of my feet. She knew, of course she knew, no wonder she'd been so coy. I'd thought she thought I was strange – not that she was hiding his death from me. It was impossible. It couldn't have happened. Not Vincent, no – I fell to my knees on and howled like a wolf, singing out my pain until I changed back into one and hurtled through the forest at full speed. My wolf liked her scent, but I was still in charge.

She'd lied to me – and if she'd caused his death, I would kill her for it.

7

After finding his clothes in the forest, I decided I'd take my chances at the airport. I packed my bag and tossed his entire cabin, looking for keys. There were two closets at the back. One of them was full of camping gear and clothing for cold weather – the other one was full of what I realized with horror were traps. At least fifty of them, all tangled up, chains ending in silent toothy metal grins. I shuddered – what the hell kind of person had all these? And why?

I closed the doors, grabbing the copy of National Geographic I'd found underneath a folded parka. His keys might be out there, in the pocket of his jeans. Maybe I should go back and try to get them?

But I heard a foot on the stair. I fell into the couch, and flipped the magazine open.

"You're back," I said as though I'd been expecting him all along. I used the voice I used to use with guys before Vincent, breathlessly excited.

"See?" he said, holding a headless rabbit up. *He's a mostly naked man who wrenches the heads off of small animals, and has the props for a horror movie in his closet. Wonderful.*

"I'll be back," he announced, grabbing a really big knife and taking it outside.

I stayed in for a moment and breathed. *Baby, I don't know why you wanted me to play Little House on the Prairie with some weirdo, but a girl's got to have standards.* My head was still on my shoulders, and I knew what to do. I'd kill him with kindness, at least until I found those keys. I steeled myself and went outside, where he was cleaning his catch.

"Is there anything I can do to help?" I stood just out of arm's reach, my chest out, my voice soft and seductive.

"Not really," he said, without looking over – until I was frowning.

"I don't like feeling useless," I said, dropping the act.

He paused to think. "You can stoke the fire. And find a can of beans in the pantry – don't worry about the expiration dates. And when we're done eating, you can take the dishes down to the creek and wash them."

"Okay," I said and nodded. It was a start. And the creek was the same direction as the truck was – maybe he was the 'leave the keys in the sunshade and the doors unlocked' type.

He gave me one tentative double-take before I went back inside.

RABBIT MEAT WAS SURPRISINGLY DELICIOUS – that, or not having eaten anything in a day'd made me hungry. I'd learned not to be picky a long time ago – you ate when you could eat with what was still open when you walked the street. I never wanted to eat Taco Bell again.

He was watching me – too closely. I stopped gnawing a rib or a leg, I didn't know, and smiled at him. *Get on his good side, Sammy.* Assuming that he had one. "This is pretty good!"

"Yeah," he agreed.

He was hard to cozy up to when all his time up here had made him forget how to talk. I didn't want to just throw myself at him again – once could be a lucky accident, twice would be setting a precedent. Instead I took my empty plate over to him, and leaned over to take his. Flash a little bit of cleavage, then I'd be off to do women's work. "I'll be right back."

He glanced at the window. "Don't bother. It's almost dark."

"It's not that far –" I protested. I didn't want to spend another night here if I didn't have to. He was stronger than I was, but once I was off in his truck he wouldn't be able to catch me.

"I'll take you there tomorrow, and make sure you know the path." He took the plate from my hand and roughly set it down.

Goddammit. I pulled away from him and he grabbed my hand – and the look he gave me just then – I recognized it. It stabbed me worse than a knife could. He was completely tortured. Scared. Lost. I knew what that look felt like inside. "Sarah – where is he?"

And maybe I'd been running from this, too – maybe more than the naked-rabbit-murdering. There was no way he wouldn't ask about Vincent eventually, and I knew I couldn't lie to him, not when he was looking at me like that. I bit my lips, trying to think of words to say that wouldn't hurt him, when I was saved from answering by the distant howl of a wolf.

"Fuck." He turned toward the window, stood, and pushed me back. "I've got to go."

"What – why?"

"No time to explain." He started for the door, and then turned and looked at me. His face was completely different now – the hurt was gone, replaced by rage and anger. I gasped.

"What's wrong?"

He lunged for me like he had the night before, too fast for me to react, and slammed a hand across my face. "Shut up."

I started screaming and didn't stop until he gagged me.

WHAT THE FUCK, *what the fuck, what the fuck* – my ankles were tied to each other and my hands were laced through the metal headboard of his shitty bed and then I heard him lock me in and leave me. I thrashed, listening to more howls in the distance – what the fuck was going on?

At first I thought he was going to – my teeth ground around the fabric he'd shoved inside my mouth. It'd happened before. It was a risk you took every time you went out on the streets. There was always some guy who thought he deserved to get what he wanted, more than you deserved control of your life.

"HOW MUCH DO you think you're worth to him?" Philly the Chicken Man asked, leering down. He'd boosted a frozen chicken delivery truck early on in his career, and after that the name stuck. It didn't match him physically, he was a musclebound 6'4", but it suited his courage just fine because here we were, inside a shipping container together, alone.

He'd yanked the gag out of my mouth so I could talk. "Come on, bitch – how much're you worth to him? You gotta know."

I didn't say anything and he hit me.

It wasn't unexpected. I wish I could lie and say it didn't hurt, but he hit me like you'd hit a man, a full fist. I could feel my jaw rattle and it made me bite my tongue. Blood welled inside my mouth – and I spit it at his feet.

He laughed at my small defiance. "That's how it's going to be?"

Philly was on the outs with the family. I didn't know the specifics, only that a deal he'd been responsible for had fallen through and others had taken it poorly.

He paced back and forth in the small room like a caged tiger, one hand in his pocket fondling his phone. He'd picked me up off the street in a van. I hadn't been paying attention because the streets didn't feel dangerous to me anymore, ever since I'd become Vincent's girl.

It'd never occurred to me that being with him might make me a target.

"He'll kill you if you don't let me go right now. Blindfold me, take me back, drop me off, and I'll ask him to let you live. He might even listen."

Philly paced the other way. "He'll kill you, he'll kill you –" he said, mocking me. "Is that your only threat?" He fished a pair of pliers out of his coat. "If he doesn't call me back soon, I'm going to pull all your teeth out and make you blow me."

I grit my teeth together and fought not to wince as my jaw wiggled.

He went for his pocket – the one with the phone – and pulled it out to look for messages and check the time. He frowned, not liking either answer, and then turned toward me.

"I guess I'll have to set my own price." His eyes narrowed. "Everyone knows what you used to be."

I stared at him with dead eyes. It didn't matter what everyone knew, only what Vincent thought.

"So you must be amazing," he said, stretching the word out with irony, "for V to think about sticking his dick in you after so many other guys got there first. Maybe I should find out and then price you myself, afterwards."

"Anything you do to me, he'll do you ten times worse to you." My voice was flat. I was ready. He wouldn't be the first, but Vincent would make sure he was the last.

"Oh yeah?" he said, coming near me.

I didn't answer him. I was already gone.

Some girls drank, some girls got high, but me – I just had a door on the inside. There was a space inside myself that I was going to fall into. People talk about happy places, visualizing beaches, listening to waves hit shore beneath a palm tree. This place was like that, only for girls like me. It was dark and it was cold and you weren't yourself there. You didn't have to be. You didn't have to be there at all.

I opened it up, and I went through.

Cold cement behind me, at head, hips, and thighs. A careless tear of fabric and then flesh moving inside other flesh.

"Oh yeah, that's gooooood –"

Time passing. Seconds or hours. It didn't matter. It didn't count.

"Say I'm better than he is." Hands on my jaw. A twinge of pain, enough to bring me back. I fought to close the door again, to get to go away.

"Say it –" he demanded, shaking me, hitting me again. I focus on him, briefly, his sweaty horrible face with his stinking breath and his awful orders. "Say it," he shouts, punctuating himself with thrusts.

I stare up at him, dead inside. "No."

He shouts something and shakes me and hits me again and I'm gone, the door's closed. I've been hurt before, but even the man I love hurts me, and I know pain can be swallowed.

The sound of rolling metal. Fresh air, a wave of dark humidity. The cessation of penetration, and the beginning of his screams.

"Sam? Sammy?"

Someone tugs me up. I'm like a rag doll, limp, arms dragging.

"Come back, Sam," Vincent says.

I look for the door inside me and the door handle slips through my fingers.

"It's safe now, Sam."

His voice pulls me through the darkness like a pipe player charms a snake.

"I've got you. I'm not letting go."

I try to blink my eyes. One's too swollen to move, and the other's doubled, seeing three of him. Reality crushes in, bruises, burns and tears, a painful final blow.

"Is he gone?" I whisper.

Vincent nods and crushes me to his chest. "Syd's got him."

I nod, and close my eyes.

I DON'T KNOW how much time passed, tied up, surrounded by cricket song.

I could find my door again if I had to. But who would bring me back? I waited, tears streaming down my face, wondering when Max would return, and what he would do when he got back.

The door to the cabin unlocked and he burst in. He was by the bed in three short strides, staring down, enraged. He reached out for my neck with both hands and I felt the span of his hands, his fingers wrapping to touch in back and in front, and knew this was it, I was going to die.

I closed my eyes and thought of Vincent as he jumped back.

"You – you," he stuttered, holding his hands to his chest like he was hugging a child. He stared at me, eyes wild, and then turned and went outside again.

What was wrong with him?

What was he going to do to me?

Minutes passed. The crickets started up again, and the door swung with a gentle breeze.

He returned a long time later without a shirt and with a resigned expression. I didn't dare say anything or move. He made a sound of strangled frustration and then ripped my clothes off of me, tearing them along their seams, like I was wearing spiderwebs not denim. And then he untied me from the bed, everything except the gag, and picked me up over his shoulder to carry me out of the cabin, completely naked.

I struggled, but he was so much stronger than I was, and faster – I couldn't hit him anywhere, his neck or knees or eyes. His arm trapped my waist on his shoulder, and his other arm held my legs down as I tried to kick him in mid-air.

He's going to take me out into the woods and hold my limbs down with traps and pull off my head like a rabbit's while he dances naked under the moon.

My head bobbed against his back and I stopped fighting – he was too strong, there was no point. All I needed to do now was concentrate on finding my door. I hadn't summoned it in so long, but I knew it hadn't gone far – it was always waiting inside me, yawning like an open mouth. All I'd have to do is let go and fall in. Vincent taught me how far I could bend and still come back – without him, all I'd have to do is let go.

It would feel just like drowning and then it'd all be over.

Max picked me up off of his shoulder and threw me. I sailed – not for the ground, but for my open door, ready to fall through at last and lock it behind me – when I landed with a splash in cold water.

The shock of the cold made my body a traitor, gasping and fighting for air. I wrestled my way up to the surface, coughing and panting, prying the gag out of my mouth.

I stroked away from the creek's edge – he stood on the bank in moonlight, and I know that he can still see me.

"Take a bath. And then come back," he said then walked away in the dark.

8

S ilver. He'd given her silver on purpose, to protect her from me –
or others like me. I went outside before I could do anything else
dumb.

My hands burned where I'd touched her necklace, and I could
feel the silver poisoning coursing inside me as my body tried to fight
it off. My wolf was confused, angry – at her for burning us, bereft by
Vincent's death, and at Karl for being Karl. It was searching for
release, and I tried to shove it down so I could think.

Karl'd said it was her fault – but if it was, why'd Vincent give her
my number? Had he been that blinded by love? I couldn't imagine
that happening. Vincent was many things, but never a fool.

It was more likely that Karl'd been lying. Not about his death –
his glee was too genuine for that – but about the circumstances that
caused it.

She knew he was dead. And as mad as I was at her for not telling
me, I couldn't blame her, now that I was sane.

If I was. Was I? I didn't know. My wolf felt awfully close – wanting
to *hunt, kill, fuck* – I could almost feel it pacing inside me, looking for
weak spots.

Part of me was tempted to give in. How many times in the past seven years had I just wanted to let all of my humanity go, turn wolf and stay that way? Let the wild side finally have me?

Only the hope of seeing him again had held me back. And now? There wasn't anything stopping me. I took all my clothes off out of habit and crouched down in the middle of my porch. All I had to do was finally let myself go, become a wolf, and disappear. Let it carry me away on its four feet from this forest to the next to the one after that – if you stayed wolf long enough, you wouldn't come back.

But what about her?

My cabin still stank of her – and him. I pushed back onto my knees and pressed my head into my hands, rocking back and forth, hovering on the verge of the change.

Inside me, my wolf gloried and cajoled, whispering simple things. *Chase, kill, fuck, chase, kill, fuck.* Life was easier as a wolf, and both of us knew it. No one tried to use a wolf, wolves never got confused. On all fours, I knew where my place was in the pack, even if it was a low one. It was only when I was a human that I felt all this agony, wanting more than I could ever get, and my wolf didn't understand why we tortured ourselves so.

I concentrated on the things I knew I could explain to him.

The pack wanted her – and *he'd* sent her to me to protect.

My wolf remembered *him.* Our old alpha, more than Syd had ever been. My lips pursed to form a howl and my blood rushed low.

Protecting her was a final order from *him*, from beyond the grave. And my wolf and I would be damned if I wouldn't see it through.

I got up and pulled my pants on. No matter how much I missed him, nothing could smell like him or her inside my house.

I DUMPED her in the creek against her protests, and the second I got back I stoked the fire in the stove. I fed her clothing to it and tried not to breathe the acrid smoke that wafted up, then dragged her bag out from underneath the bed.

Another set of underwear – tossed into the fire. The wig she'd worn – I'd dump it in the creek tomorrow, burning it would make the stove stink too bad. Her robe – I tore into shreds and shoved in.

There was cash and ID – I could bury them. I knew how to do it right, so no one would be able to find it but me.

The bag itself? Had to go. I held it open and leaned my head in, breathing deep. It would be the last time I would smell him. With a strangled sound, I pulled it apart at the zipper-seams – and a book fell out of the bottom.

I picked it up. It was a small notebook, and every page was full of Vincent's handwriting. I immediately flipped to the front.

"Samantha – I don't know where you'll be when you find this, but I hope you're safe.

If you're gone, stay gone. If you're not gone yet – go. As fast as you can. Get out of town and never come back. Pretend that you're being chased by wolves, okay? Run and keep running. Don't look back.

I want you to be happy, Sam. Start over somewhere new and when you're safe drop this in the mail three states over from wherever it is you are, so they can't trace you. Call the number below and send it to the US Marshall who answers – I've been working with him. I'm so sorry I couldn't tell you. I promise we were supposed to get out together. I never wanted to leave you in this world alone.

Be safe, Sammy. For both of us.

I love you.

V."

I KNELT THERE, holding the testament to how much he trusted her – Samantha, I realized now, not Sarah like she'd said – in my hands. I was glad I hadn't killed her, and so jealous of what she'd had with him it felt like silver in my heart.

VINCENT and I were driving away from a botched deal and I was bleeding into the upholstery of his car.

"Take me home," I said, leaning against the door. My home had been his home now for a year.

"I'm taking you to the doctor." His voice was clipped, he'd seen me get shot.

I ground my teeth together. "You don't need to."

"He's one of us, he'll treat you off the books –" Vincent went on, taking turns that drove us further away from our house.

"No. Take me home."

"I'm not going to watch you die, okay? I don't care if I go to jail – we've got lawyers, we pay them enough –" he took the next turn angry, and I grunted when I hit the door. Hands slippery with blood found the handle.

This was it. I was going to have to leave him now, for his own good. I should have never gotten involved with a human, not as deep as this. I'd have to run, let him assume I'd died, that was the only way to get out of this without telling him what I was and exposing him to danger.

One of his hands reached over from the steering wheel and grabbed my knee. "I care about you, Max." He glanced over at me, and I could see the terror in his eyes – he thought that he was losing me.

Was he?

I didn't want to endanger him. But I wasn't ready to give him up yet either.

"Pull over."

He looked at me. "Fuck no – we've got to –"

I took his hand in mine. "Pull over."

He yanked his hand back and twisted the steering wheel until we were idling beside the road. "If you think I'm going to let you die –" he started, whirling on me.

"Did you ever have a secret so big you could never tell anyone?"

He stared at me like bloodloss had made me insane. Of course he had secrets, he was in the family.

I inhaled. "I'm gonna be fine."

"I saw you get shot. I'm not an idiot."

"The bullet went through me." I could feel the exit wound it'd left, if I reached around with one hand.

"So?"

"I'll heal up. Like I always do."

"It went through you Max. Who knows what it hit. Peritonitis is no way to go."

"I'll be fine." I sat straighter up in the seat. The moon was half-full overhead. Under its silver gaze, I was already healing.

His eyes were dark by the light of the dashboard. He knew I healed fast, he'd talked about it before, but what I was saying pressed his definitions of reality.

This was the moment I'd been dreading ever since I'd taken up with him. I'd conned myself into believing it'd never happen, and had turned myself into a fool.

We were at a juncture. Leave now for his own good – or stay for mine.

Inside me, my wolf whined. He was the only person I'd ever loved. I couldn't go, no matter how much I knew I ought to. Maybe if I were more like him, I'd be that strong, but I was just me – and I knew he'd have to ask.

"How do you know you'll be all right?"

I swallowed. "You won't want to believe me when I tell you."

An eyebrow quirked. "You're an alien?" he said, dryly, his hands wringing the steering wheel.

"Worse. A werewolf."

He barked a laugh. "What kind of shitty joke is that?"

I looked at him completely calmly. "I mean what I said."

He twisted his whole body to face me. "Prove it."

"I just survived a gutshot that hit my liver. What else do you need?" I held up my shirt. The entry wound was already shrinking, soon it'd be like it hadn't been there at all. He reached a tentative finger out to touch the hole it'd left, like I had stigmata.

His eyes met mine again. "Show me."

I shook my head. "No." If I showed him my wolf – there were rules, and then there were *rules*. But I was cornered – and he wasn't used to being told no. It was my own fault, I encouraged him to boss me. "It's why I'm gone three nights a month. I have to hunt with my pack."

"There are others like you?"

I closed my eyes and sighed. Maybe I had had some blood loss after all. "I shouldn't have said anything. The punishment for telling a human is death – for you, and me."

He stared at me in wonder as I put my shirt back down. "All those times – those fights – no wonder I felt invincible around you."

I smiled softly. "Not invincible. Just harder to kill." I tried to read his face, to see if I saw his opinion changing. "You can never tell anyone. You have to take the secret to your grave."

"I will. I swear it."

"Good." I knew he'd be true to his word. No one would even torture it out of him.

"I just – I can't believe it. Are you sure that you can't show me?"

"Yeah. But –" I licked my lips and his eyes met mine again. There was something different there now. He wasn't scared – and he still wanted me. When he looked at me like that, all my blood sank, getting ready. "Maybe there's something I can show you."

He nodded eagerly.

"Take me home, first."

VINCENT DROVE MORE CAUTIOUSLY up to our house. He kept looking at me like I might go away, and I kept worrying. It'd seemed like a good idea at the time – but what if he changed his mind?

What had I done? Telling him about us – even if there was no reason for him to tell another living soul, and no one would believe him if he did – it was such a huge risk, such a completely bad idea – he put the car into park, and without saying a word, both of us walked inside. He followed me into the bathroom.

"I want to see the rest," he said, looking meaningfully at the bloodstain on my shirt.

I turned my back to him and lifted it off. He made a surprised sound, and then I felt him touching me. I wanted to lean back into his arms and let him hold me, push me against the wall and –

"You really are –" he whispered.

I swallowed my thoughts. "I really am." I angled myself in the mirror so I could see what he saw. I was bloody around the exit wound, but it was healing, and the entry wound was almost gone. "I'm going to take a shower, and let Mother Nature finish up." I reached into the shower and turned the hot water on.

"Sure," Vincent said, and kicked his shoes off.

I tilted my head. "What're you –"

"I saw you thinking about leaving in the car." His hands went for the top button of his shirt. He was spattered with my blood.

I leaned against the cold glass of the shower door. "I didn't go."

"But you thought about it." His eyes were serious as he went for the next button, and the one below that.

I nodded.

His shirt was open and he slipped it off, letting it fall. "I don't want you to leave me, Max. I don't want you to even think about leaving me."

I closed my eyes and let the words wash over me. It was everything I'd ever wanted to hear. The risk of him knowing was worth the reward of being known for who I was – and feeling like this.

When I opened my eyes up again he was smiling softly at me, and he stepped near. "Show me what you want to show me, I'm not going anywhere."

All of me, wolf and human, thrilled. I'd been holding back for months, every time I came, wanting – aching – to knot. I started breathing heavy, and the steam from the shower fogged us both as he started kissing me.

I pushed his pants off of him as he pushed mine off of me, and we danced into the shower together, hands eagerly searching one another's bodies, him pressing my back into the cold tile wall as his tongue moved inside my mouth, making me moan. I could feel his erection rubbing against my thigh and reached for it, pulling one wet hand down his length as he reached his hands down to hold my ass and pull my hips close. My erection rubbed against his stomach and I thrust without thinking, wanting more for it there. I took one of his hands and put it on my cock. He started stroking me between us as his other hand's fingers teased the edge of my asshole, getting me ready to take him. The pink-tinged water'd started to run clear, I knew I was whole, I could show him, it was safe –

I pushed him back so that he stood directly under the water streaming down from above, and I stroked myself for him, in front of him. I wanted him to see it – I was scared to show it – I'd been hiding it for so long – my eyes were closed and I was biting my lips – trying so hard to relax and let go –

His hand met mine, taking over, and I moaned, opening my eyes again.

"Don't stop. No matter what," I whispered, and he nodded, sensing how important this was for me. He knelt down, still stroking, and lowered his head to lick my balls.

"Oh God –" I whispered, as his tongue lapped between my balls and my leg, and then licked up the seam of my sack, as his hand kept stroking. My hips arched forward to give him more of me, any part he would touch or taste, and he moved his head to let me thrust into his mouth. I stayed there, frozen for a second, as his tongue lapped up my precum and swirled around my head. "Yes –" I panted, my hips rocking, his hands and mouth moving in time. I needed release – but I needed one more thing worse –

It was safe. He was mine. I was his. We were together. I'd spent so long holding back to protect the both of us that it'd become second nature to me.

Please, I begged my body, and my wolf whined.

I looked down, and saw him staring up, watching me struggle. He pulled back. "Come for me, Max," he ordered. At the sound of his command, my knot flared at the base of my cock, swelling out. He gasped – and then took me into his mouth again and sucked me harder.

I came and I came and I came, shooting all of my cum into his mouth, shouting unintelligible things. He kept stroking and sucking until I was completely done – my balls had never felt so empty, even if my cock was still hard.

I sank down the wall as I crashed back to earth, and he folded in next to me, hot water still pouring down. He leaned against me and kept his free hand on my knot, at the base of my cock where I was swollen, meant to lock me to the one I loved. "What is this?" he asked, marveling.

I looked down at my mating knot being held by the man I adored. I wanted to keep him there forever.

"It's –" I flushed, not sure how to explain it to someone not of my kind. "It's what happens when – when you're with the right person."

He made a wise noise, stroking me. I didn't know my knot would make me stay so hard, or feel so good whenever he touched it. I felt exposed, but not ashamed. This was who I'd always wanted to be with him.

"Have you gotten it with others?" he asked.

My breath hitched. I didn't want to lie, not when he'd accepted all my other truths. "No," I said, just a whisper.

He made an even wiser noise, and moved his mouth back on my cock.

9

I stayed in the creek until I thought I'd get hypothermia. Goddamn him, what gave him the right to act like this? I slapped an open palm against the water – and found the night was even colder when I got out.

I had money, and I had ID, and at least one clean pair of underwear left – I'd go up there, get my bag, and then go, just go.

I stumbled in the dark, my feet being poked and prodded by turned stones and the roots of trees. I got back, and saw the fire inside the cabin burning brighter than ever and paused. I'd floated. I hoped he wouldn't think that made me a witch.

I got to the door and hauled it open. He looked over his shoulder at me, his face guilty. He still didn't have a shirt on – what the hell was his problem with clothing?

"I need my things and then I'm going." I'd walk out of here naked if I had to, I didn't need a goddamned thing from him anymore.

"Stay," he said, voice firm. I looked at him, and he at me. "We both know you don't have anywhere else."

I bit my lips together. "You heard he's gone, didn't you."

"Yeah."

I sank down to my knees. The smoke smelled awful, but at least the fire was warm. "How?"

"I can't tell you."

Sure, why not. I sunk my head, and then looked around for my robe to cover myself with. He went and got a sweater from his non-serial-killer closet for me and brought it back, handing it over. I tugged it on. It was huge, hanging past my waist to bunch on the floor. It smelled like he did, musky and good. I pulled out my necklace to sit on it between my breasts and glint in the firelight.

"You were his, weren't you." The odd way he said it made me look at him.

"Yeah." He was studying me intently, the way Vincent sometimes did – used to – and then I remembered the prior night when I'd fucked him. "Oh, God – you must think I'm a whore." I had been, but –

"No. I know what it's like to trade sex for safety." His eyes glazed over like he was seeing his past not mine. "I should have known better. I should have pushed you away –"

"You couldn't have known." I untucked and retucked my legs to be more comfortable, and hid my hands inside their sleeves. That hadn't been exactly what I was doing, but better for him to think that. "How did you know Vincent?"

"We were lovers." He watched me for a reaction. "You're not surprised?"

I shook my head. "I knew every part about him. Even that one. We didn't have secrets. He was very clear about that. From the first day we met. He made me swear." Which was why I'd been so surprised there was only one go-bag there. I frowned, and pulled my legs up underneath the sweater, until it enveloped me. "How long were you with him?"

"Three years. You?"

It seemed best to be truthful. "Seven."

"Did he ever...mention me?"

I couldn't help but hear the hopeful tone in his voice – but now was not the time for lies. "No. I'm sorry."

"Don't be."

The way he was staring into the fire, looking lost, broke my heart. "Did you love him?"

He nodded.

"I loved him too."

"I know. And if he didn't love you, you wouldn't be here." He stoked the fire. I saw the tail of something blue curl inside it as it blackened.

"What was that?"

"Your robe, clothes, and backpack. Don't worry – I saved the money and your ID."

"What?" I crawled toward the fire. "You burned – my things? Why?"

"You wouldn't understand."

"But –" I looked from him to the flames. "That was all I had. All I had of him – my time with him –" I reached out, like I could snatch a piece of it back.

"Not all of it." He put a book into my open hand. "He left this for you, Samantha."

He knew my name now – I snatched the book back protectively. I hadn't packed it – Vincent must have, when he'd given up on his own bag. I opened it, reading by the light of the fire.

"SAMANTHA – *I don't know where you'll be when you find this, but I hope you're safe.*

If you're gone, stay gone. If you're not gone yet – go. As fast as you can. Get out of town and never come back. Pretend that you're being chased by wolves, okay? Run and keep running. Don't look back.

I want you to be happy, Sam. Start over somewhere new and when you're safe drop this in the mail three states over from wherever it is you are, so they can't trace you. Call the number below and send it to the US Marshall who answers – I've been working with him. I'm so sorry I couldn't tell you. I promise we were supposed to get out together. I never wanted to leave you in this world alone.

Be safe, Sammy. For both of us.
I love you.
V."

THE REST of the pages were a list – of addresses and names, dates and dollar amounts. I thumbed through it quickly – almost all of them were full. I sank back and my stomach dropped as I read on.

"Have you ever seen that before?" Max asked.

I shook my head.

"Is that what I think it is?" his voice was low.

"The reason he got killed? Yeah," I said, my voice small. I riffled through the pages again. Vincent was so safe, and so careful – and so thorough. How had he gotten caught? "He – it'd –" I inhaled and exhaled, trying to put my thoughts into words. "The family changed. I mean, they were never good guys, you know? I'm not an idiot, I could see that. But things were getting worse. The violence – it isn't that it wasn't safe, it was never safe, but they were taking bigger risks for less reward – they weren't watching each other's backs like they used too – he told me it was becoming less like a family, and more like a gang. I knew he didn't like that, but I had no idea it'd come to this." I hefted the book cataloguing Vincent's betrayal. "He was trying to bring it back, make it better, but the others wouldn't listen to him –"

The signs had all been there, looking back. Hell, us even making go-bags, talking about how we'd escape – why hadn't I realized it sooner? This book was the result of weeks of effort – how had he kept it hidden from me all that time? Was I blind, or just stupid?

"Who else knew?"

"No one. He never said anything when anyone else was around. And I would have taken it to the grave." I stopped questioning everything Vincent had done and tried to remember if I'd ever given any of his dissatisfaction away. I'd always done my best to never talk to Syd, and I didn't interact with most of the rest of the family, they were all too 'good' for me.

I just wish I'd known. I knew he'd done it to protect me, but –
how lonely he must have been, without anyone else to turn to –
without anyone else at the very end –

Oh God, Vincent, baby, why. For the first time, I really felt that he
was gone. I started crying, and all the tears I hadn't let myself shed in
the past twenty four hours welled up.

I set the book down and sobbed.

Max reached over and patted my back, like someone completely
unused to the act. It made me realize what I was missing more and
cry harder, and then he made a sad sound too. Without asking for
permission he grabbed me – how the fuck was he so strong? – and
pulled me underneath one of his arms, pressing my head against his
chest. I didn't fight him, I clung to him and he to me, like we were one
another's life preservers in a storm-tossed ocean. His chest rumbled
and the sounds he made were just as sad as mine.

I didn't know how much time passed, only that he recovered
before I did, and started stroking my hair, rocking me softly. After all
the being afraid of him, there was nothing but gentleness now.
When I could manage to talk again, I pulled back, and he quickly let
me go.

"If I didn't know – then who did? And how?"

"That's not what you should be asking yourself, Sam." His gaze
was serious as he looked at me. "He wanted a different life for you –
he bought it with his own." He rocked up to standing and went for
the safe closet again and hauled a new bag out of it. "I'm taking you
out of town tomorrow."

"What?" My tone surprised the both of us. It was exactly what I'd
wanted less than an hour ago.

"It's the reason he sent you here. He knew I'd get you out safely."
Max's face looked resolved, moving from the tenderness he'd shown
with me back to the glowering man I'd known so far.

"But – what'll you do?"

"What do you mean?"

"Are you – just going to stay here?" I didn't want to ask him to
come with me, but I didn't want to be alone. Plus – the way he was

moving, the far-away look in his eyes – "You're going to do something. I can tell."

"I am," he admitted. "After you're gone."

"What?"

"The less you know the better."

I stared at him. "Did you really just fucking tell me that?"

He looked like I'd slapped him, but didn't answer me. I stood up and started shouting. "It's his fault! He promised me a life without secrets! He told me that he trusted me – and he made me trust him! I didn't want to, but he made me – and now – and he held this back from me –" I pointed at the book.

"That doesn't change the fact that you're leaving tomorrow."

"Even if you make me get on a plane, I'll be flying right back." I stared up at him. "You can't make me be safe. No one can. If my life has had one guiding principle – it's that."

"He wanted you to be safe," Max said, like that would change my mind.

"Fuck what he wanted – he's not here to see it." He was standing by the fire, its light giving him shadows that made him look unholy. It lit his hair like a halo, but the shadowed expression on his face was grim and cruel. His naked chest heaved, there were scars slashed upon it, and I imagined Vincent stroking them, his hands pressing into all the secret places of Max's body like he had mine.

We were one and the same, Max and I. We had to be.

I took a step, and then another step, until I was standing right in front of him and I put both my hands on his chest and stared up as he watched me cautiously. "I want revenge, Max. Whoever found out, whoever told on him, whoever got him killed – I want revenge. When they're dead, I'll go, but not a second sooner." I kneaded the muscles of his chest as though I were a cat. "I can't live my life without him, knowing that they're still alive."

He swayed under my hands, as though the current of my hatred was passing through to him.

Knowing Vincent had touched him, cherished him – maybe even loved him – made me feel like he would understand. And he was the only other person on the planet who knew what losing Vincent felt like.

"We might die," he finally said.

"So?" I asked, completely sincerely.

He closed his eyes and bent his head down. Then, faster than I could see, he reached forward and grabbed my hair, pulling my head down so that I was showing him my neck. I was scared in the way someone who sees a snake is startled – one moment you're fine, the next you're not – as he controlled all of me, making me sway. If I swatted at him or pushed him or complained, all of this would be over, I knew it, and so I rocked with him, letting him pull me in, feeling his breath along my neck, even as my hands on his chest felt him breathe it. Time slowed to a crawl as he weighed my resolve versus my fear.

"All right," he said, releasing me. I took an unsteady step back and put my hands down. Primal urges rolled through my body – I wanted to be taken like that, like there was no question of who was in charge or who I was supposed to be. I shoved them down as he went on. "We need a plan."

"Anything. I'm in." I swallowed, and held my hand out. He looked from me to it and took it, shaking it firmly. The look in his eyes just then – wild, angry, and determined – made me very glad that he and I were on the same side.

10

He was right to mate with her, after me. She didn't know what the firelight did to her, how it ran over her body like electricity – and when she touched me, how it burned. It was like she had a core of silver underneath her curves – maybe she'd been soft, once, but living with Vincent and dealing with the family, had made the right parts of her like steel. The tears she'd shed – we'd shed – earlier, were gone, replaced by a lust for revenge, and who could blame her? I'd had seven years to come to grips with Vincent's absence, she'd had only a little over a day.

And when she'd let me pull her near to make sure she wouldn't break – the wolf inside me *shivered*.

"We have to figure out who to kill first." My truck keys were in my pockets – I didn't go to the closet for a shirt, in fact I needed to ditch these pants, they smelled like her and him. "You read that book and try to figure it out, and I'll be back later – I'm going out to try to get us answers."

"Where?"

"The bars, the clubs – the places where people talk."

"And you think they'll talk to you?"

"They'd better." I took two strides toward the door, and she ran after me.

"Don't you dare lock me in."

"Not tonight. But do not leave here. Trust me, this forest isn't safe."

She nodded, and I believed her. "What about your clothes?" she asked me, as I stepped off the porch.

"What about them?" I asked back, and went into the darkness.

Truth was, I'd hidden stockpiles of clothes and cheap boots several places in the forest. Never knew when or where I'd be in wolf form and quickly need to appear human. I stripped off my jeans outside when I was far enough away from the cabin, turned into a wolf, and picked up the keys I'd dropped with my teeth. Then I ran for a cache and changed back into human, so nothing on me would smell like her.

The pack wouldn't be happy to see me, but they were the only place I could start. I circled below the ridge down to my truck, and got in.

I was with Vincent when I got the call.

"We're going to take your place."

I'd noticed pack members ingratiating themselves with the family, I couldn't not. I was on the gravy train, so of course they wanted in too. Working security and muscle was a hell of a lot easier than being a construction worker as a were. It wasn't 9-5, they expected you to be up at night, and you got to be as intimidating as you wanted to.

I just didn't want to think they'd go this far.

"You have to leave."

I stared around at the room I'd grown accustomed to, the chairs, the wide leather couch, and Vincent, lounging with his legs across mine, a book in one hand and a glass of wine in the other.

"When?" I asked.

"Immediately," the voice on the other end of the line said, and hung up.

Vincent looked up as I brought the phone down. "What's wrong?"

Ever since I'd exposed myself to him, I'd been dreading this possible moment. Our life together'd been so perfect – he knew me and I knew him, and we knew *all* of each other. It wasn't fair that I had to go – but the pack had never been fair where I was concerned.

"I need to leave," I said slowly.

"Why? Where?"

"My time's up." I started pushing his legs off of me.

"What the fuck, Max – this isn't funny."

How thick were the walls and how close were my packmembers? If I didn't leave now, they'd kill us both on principle.

"You know what it's like to get orders, Vincent." My hands reached for his. "I just got mine."

"But – why?"

I reached over and put a hand on his lips before he could say anything incriminating. I pointed to my lips and spoke without sound. *If I disobey them, they'll kill me.*

His eyes narrowed. *We have guns.*

If you try anything, they'll kill you too.

I'd never told Vincent about the pack's infiltration. I'd been trying so hard to keep him safe – the less I told him the better. But now there was no time.

You can't trust anyone new. Look around on a full moon. You know why they're not there.

He bent over, and grabbed my head, pull me close to him. *We can fight them.*

I knew that he'd loved me then, even if he'd never said it. The tortured look in his eyes, knowing he was losing me. *There's no fighting what you are,* I told him, kissed him, and walked out the door.

I PUT the car in park outside of The Doghouse. It was Syd's chosen dive, first for the name, secondly because the bartender poured strong. Someone was supposed to be guarding Vincent the night he'd been killed – I wanted to find out who.

I rolled in and the first person I saw was Syd. I saw Syd-the-wolf every full moon night, as I skulked around the edges of the pack, begging for a place at whatever we'd killed. I hadn't seen Syd-the-man in years.

"Well, well," he said, turning around the second he scented me. "If it isn't the mountain man."

I walked straight for him. "Who was protecting him that night?"

He frowned at me. "Who told you?"

"Karl." I didn't care if he got in trouble. Fuck him.

Karl came down the hall from the bathroom, adjusting himself. "Aw, shit," he said, seeing me.

"You went and told him our business?" Syd asked, without turning around.

"I was hoping he knew where the bitch was hiding out. Maybe he and Vinnie fucked there years ago or something." He shrugged one shoulder.

"His name was Vincent, not Vinnie," I corrected, under my breath. Syd and Karl were the only weres in here. The rest of the men present were family men of assorted caliber. I recognized some of them, and knew some of them recognized me.

"He's dead now, and I'll call him whatever I want."

I ignored him and looked at Syd again. "I need to know who was supposed to be there."

"Why?"

"Why the fuck do you think?" I said. His eyes narrowed. There was a line coming up. My wolf was whispering not to cross it, don't run over, run-back, hide, but I didn't give a fuck if I made my alpha mad anymore.

"Let it go, Maxie," Karl said, reaching out to push me back. I knew what he was thinking, we were in public, this was no place to make a scene. "You going to take on the whole family? On your own? These things happen, Max. He had a good string. Let it go."

I was shivering in rage. It'd been so long since I'd been among their number as a man. All the times they'd been cruel, all the scars they'd left on me, inside and out, came rushing up. On full moon nights my wolf just *was*, it didn't have to deal with all the ignominy, it knew its place.

Whereas human me – my hands curled into fists. "Anyone in the family would be a fool to let you watch their back." I said it loud enough for everyone in the room to hear.

Syd growled. I knew it was coming, and I didn't care. He punched me in the stomach, and I took it like a man would, folding in and falling back. Tables scattered behind me. Other men jumped and stood, not complaining – they wanted to watch.

I grinned at Syd. I'd caught him – he'd started in here – he'd have to finish it in here. He and Karl weren't strong enough as humans to get me out the door, and there were too many witnesses for either of them to go were.

"Where were you? Where the fuck were you?" I yelled, clutching my stomach, like he'd hurt me, making a show. "You were supposed to be guarding him!" I howled, making as much of a scene as I could.

Karl made a wild noise and accepted my challenge. He grabbed a chair, unseating its owner, and ran for me.

After that we were a tangle of blows. Wood crunched overhead, punches that would have shattered a normal man's jaw, ribs, sternum. I gave as good as I got, staying upright and always in bounds, us playing a game with each other right in front of men who watched from the sidelines with glittering eyes. This was a family fight, for them and for us, they weren't going to get involved.

Karl was slower than I remembered. He was older than me and easier to harry, I got in twice as many blows on his doughy body as he did mine.

Whereas Syd was still one muscular slab of a man, underneath seven years of softer living. There was a reason he was still our alpha after all this time. The look in his eyes – challenging him here I'd taken my life into my hands, and but for the rules of the pack he'd wring it out of me.

I was chipping away at him though, one punch at a time. My wolf stirred, panicked and ecstatic in turns. Could I beat him? If I did, what would that make me? Blood raced through me, dripping out my broken nose, running out of cuts up and down my body, ringing inside my ears. Blood – and hope.

And then JD, Mike, and Georgie came through the door – enough to overwhelm me and carry me outside, one were to each of my limbs.

11

I thumbed through the book by the light of the nearest oil lamp. I recognized all the names in it – Vincent had told me everything, and reading his notes made it feel like he was whispering to me again. There were deaths listed, the locations of bodies and tossed guns, details that only someone on the inside would know.

And some of the pages were dog-eared.

In all of Vincent's books – and he'd had a lot of them – he'd never bent the corner of a single page. That was all me, I was the dog-earrer and spine-breaker, the one who put things that weren't bookmarks, like remote controls and coasters, into books to hold my place.

I wondered if it were some code. I wanted it to be – I'd take all the messages from beyond the grave from him that I could get. I went from page to page carefully to see what they had in common.

JD, Mike, Georgie, Syd – there were nine of them in all, all of them bodyguards I'd run into more than once. Syd practically lived with us, much to Vincent's chagrin – although I would admit to having been happy he was there that night with Philly the Chicken Man. Him offering to let me watch him beat Philly to death had seemed downright chivalrous at the time.

There were dollar amounts and deals underneath all of their

names, crossmatched with other names. Were they...embezzling? Syd
was in for over a hundred thousand dollars – if they were aggregate, a
gang within the family, like some sort of internal parasite – the family
ought to know. I didn't owe them any allegiance though – it was their
war with the Carminos that'd gotten Vincent killed. Or was it?
Anyone whose name was in this book had a reason to see Vincent
dead.

I flipped through it again and again, and it was like he was there
with me, just a little. I could hear his words in his voice and it was like
he was holding my hand.

Comforted by memories, I drifted off to sleep.

THERE WAS a knock at the door and I winced. This time of night, it
had to be Ray – even the most desperate of men were usually asleep
by five in the morning.

"Go away," Jesse muttered, flinging an arm out.

Good. Let her get in trouble, not me. I huddled underneath the
covers. If he was just looking for someone to hit on, he'd start in on
whoever was nearest the door.

The knock was louder now – and it didn't stop. It wasn't like the
door was locked – Ray knew that. I'd say it was a mind game, only
Ray didn't have a mind, just brute strength and the will to use it.

"Said go away!" Jesse muttered, twice as loud.

"Hey," a voice on the far side said. Jesse sat up – so did Rae and
Karen and I. The cops?

Cops didn't knock – they kicked. No matter – Karen had the
window open and was already throwing her belongings into the
alley.

The voice had sounded like – it couldn't be – "Sammy – are you in
there?"

I blinked. "Vincent?" I said, too quiet for him to hear me.

The door opened, right into Jesse's mattress – our private security
alarm and barricade. She screamed in terror and I heard him sigh.

I hopped out of my bed – I was still on the top bunk, the right of a 'top earner' according to Ray, but I wouldn't hold my place long – not without Vincent as a 'client' anymore. He hadn't told me why he'd stopped seeing me and why the hotel room was up, but I thought I knew why. I mean, there were no guarantees with us, right? I'd never asked for any – there was no point. My choices had been to get my heart broken then-now, or now-later. I'd gone with later and –

"Sammy, are you in there?"

"Vincent?" I asked again, louder.

"Thank God." There was relief in his voice, and he shoved the door harder.

I went to the door's edge to help him, stepping over a glaring Jessica, feeling silly in just a t-shirt and underwear. "What're you doing?"

"What does it look like I'm doing?" he said with a grin, shoving a bag through the door to me. "Get your things."

I took the bag, staring at him. "Why?"

"Because I've come to take you home."

I stood there, blinking. "What?"

"Get your things."

Had I heard him right?

He leaned against the door, making as much space for himself as he could. "Come on – let's go."

"But –" I looked down at the empty bag and then back to him.

"I know this isn't like the movies – and I'm sorry that I didn't catch you all having a pillow fight or something – but come on," he said beckoning me with a hand. "Ray's not going to stay down forever, and I'd like to go to sleep still tonight – after fucking you senseless."

He grinned recklessly at me and the part of me I'd been trying to deny for months, that this past week had shattered, was reborn and soared. I tossed his bag back to him – mine was already packed. I got it and wedged it and myself out into the hallway. His hand found mine and he started pulling me along.

"But what happened?"

"He wanted to charge more." Vincent said, as we reached the

living room of our cramped apartment. Ray was slumped on the floor, with a bruise the size of Vincent's fist against his jaw. "It was never you, Samantha," he said, reaching over to grab my hips and pick me up over Ray's comatose form. "He's surprisingly well connected. It took me a week to get permission to beat the shit out of him for over-charging – and as for taking you – I didn't ask."

I snorted, looking around at the small room – it was shitty, but familiar, with its faded couch and ashtrays piled high with cigarettes. Outside the open door however, was unknown.

"So what now?"

"Now – you'll come and be with me."

"At a hotel?" I guessed, suddenly feeling my lack of pants and bra.

"No. At my place. If you want to go. I assumed," he said, and looked at Ray. "You're not trading him for me, if that's what you're asking."

"Then what are you offering?" I asked, because I desperately wanted to hear him say it.

"Move in with me. Be with me. All the time. I want to know what you're thinking in the middle of the night. I want to open my heart to you. No secrets between us. Can you handle that?"

"I can!" shouted someone from the other room, and then there was snickering, and I was laughing and crying at the same time and Vincent was looking pleased and I leapt into his arms.

"I can too," I said, and he grabbed my hand and pulled me out the door and into his car. I got into the passenger side and he got into the driver side and as he drove away I honked the horn to let everyone back there know what'd happened, to say good-bye to that place and everyone in it, to let the neighbors know, the street know, the sky know, that I was finally free.

I sat up in bed in the cabin's darkness, the sound of a honking horn still echoing in my mind. Vincent's? It'd sounded so real –

Another longer honk that wasn't ending. It sounded like something had fallen against the steering wheel and it didn't stop. Oh no –

I put on my shoes, the last thing Max hadn't burned, and grabbed a flashlight. I walked back behind the cabin, the flashlight's beam spotting me, and saw Max's truck parked below.

"Max?" I called out. No one answered.

I got down the ridge as fast as I could, almost taking the last third of it on my ass, as rocks skittered out from underneath me. I reached the driver side door and opened it up. He was slouched over – I used two hands to push him back.

What the hell had happened to him? He was covered in blood, in bruises, and things that looked like bite marks criss-crossed his arms.

"Oh God, oh God," I leaned in and tried to feel for a pulse in the sticky red beneath his jaw. My finger pushed into a hole and I screamed without thinking, like a girl in a horror film. His head fluttered at the sound.

"You're alive?" I whispered. He'd made it here somehow, barely. Shit.

I watched his chest until I saw him take a breath – and heard half of it whistle out the hole in his trachea.

"Shit-shit-shit."

911 was not an option, my burner phone didn't have signal up here and even if I did I wouldn't know how to tell them where we were. It was up to me or God at this point, and I didn't give either of us very good odds.

"It's going to be okay, baby," I said, stroking his bloody hair out of his face. If he was going to die, I didn't want him to think he was alone. He'd gone out there looking for answers and they'd done this to him. Who knew what they would have done to me in his stead. "This is where you belong, okay? You're home, baby. You're home. Just stay here."

I took the flashlight back up the ridge with me and into the cabin, and pulled out everything soft I could think of, piles of sweaters and coats from his closet, and pulled the sheets off of the bed. Then I threw or dragged them down the ridge with me, so that I could make some sort of pallet for him on the ground.

"Come on. Let's get you out of there," I said, the flashlight pinched under one arm, watching for his chest to rise and fall. I pulled on his arm and prayed that it wouldn't fall off, holding tighter against the slickness of so much blood. He collapsed out of the truck and almost onto me, as I tried to direct him to the pile of moth eaten sweaters.

"Okay." I talked for my sake, not his, and was glad for the darkness, because if I could only see what the flashlight was showing me, I didn't know about the rest at that time. I could look at an arm without thinking of how his leg looked ruined, or his legs without thinking about that gaping hole in his neck. I tore sheets into strips of bandages and tied off wounds that I thought were still seeping, knowing the whole time that nothing I did was going to work, there weren't enough sheets in the world to keep his blood inside him.

I didn't see his eyes open, but I heard him whisper my name. "Sam."

I moved up his body with the flashlight and blinded us both. I dropped to kneeling by his bloody head, where it looked like someone had tried to peel his scalp off with a can opener. His eyes closed against the brightness of the light, and didn't open again. "Max – it's Sammy. I'm here." I looked for some part of him that I could squeeze to let him know that I was all right, thanks to him. And that I'd watch over him until this was over. He wouldn't be alone when he died, not like my Vincent had been. "I never should have lied to you, okay? I didn't mean to. You know how it is, for people like us. You assume you have to until you're so used to it you don't even question it anymore, you know?" I leaned over him, blotting at him with a wad of already blood-saturated cloth. "But it's Sammy, I'm here, and I'm not going anywhere."

I took his hand in mine and turned the flashlight off since it wasn't doing either of us any good. I closed my eyes and listened to the sound of all the crickets and the whistling at his neck.

Adrenaline kept me up for what felt like an hour. I had no concept of time with only the stars slowly spinning overhead and the crossing moon. The whistling sound beside me lessened, fading gently like a train running off into the night. Max was going away and there was nothing I could do. I let go of his hand and stayed with him. I didn't want any bears or mountain lions dragging him off in the night.

I'm ashamed to say that somehow without meaning to I slept.

I WOKE up alone and covered in blood.

"Oh. My. God." The nest I'd made was as covered in it as I was. Somehow a bear had to have gotten past me and taken him and dragged him off into the forest to eat. How the fuck had I slept through that? I stood, looking down at myself in horror. How was I going to bury him? I'd hear the sound of his neck whistling until the end of my days – I spun in the woods, looking in all directions, stunned and horrified, before clambering back up the ridge to the cabin.

I had to get my head on straight. Make a list. Do one thing at a time. Clean up. Get the book. Get out of here.

But I'd as good as sent him to his death, telling him we needed our revenge. What the fuck had I been thinking, saying things like that to a man like him? The life Vincent lead had always had an expiration date, but Max had been out of things until I'd pulled him back. *Oh God, oh God, oh God* – no wonder Vincent had turned, if being responsible for other people's lives had felt like this.

I fell to my knees at the top of the ridge, nauseous and out of breath – and I saw a rock clearly smeared with blood.

I got my feet under myself again, and saw a trail of it, leading to the cabin's porch. I ran for its open door.

Max was laying on the floor, sprawled out. Enough daylight filtered through the dirty windows that I could see the dried smears of blood – and his chest rise and fall.

"Max?" I ran over to where he was, looking down. How had he – he wasn't whistling anymore – his neck – the torn muscles of his arm that I knew I'd felt last night while squeezing on him to pull – I took all of him in, my mind whirling, trying to figure out what'd happened again and again, always coming up blank.

He was here now and he needed help. I latched onto that, and bent over to blow on the stove's fire and add more kindling, then ran with the kettle to the creek.

Maybe he'd just had some really shitty wounds that'd bled a lot, like when you were a kid and you scraped your knee – it looked bad, but it wasn't bad, you know? I could almost convince myself of that, that the wounds I'd seen on him last night were part of an awful dream, but then seeing him again – covered in blood, even if he wasn't still actively bleeding – I was no stranger to violence, and I wasn't dumb. I put the kettle on the stove and tore a shirt of his into washcloth portions and started to scrub him clean.

There were still wounds underneath his assorted scabs. Whatever had attacked him – it'd tried to tear him open. Like with teeth. Some of the family had fighting dogs – had they thrown him into a pit to take his chances? But the jaw span – there were divots on his arm that I could put my hand inside. A dog with a jaw wider than my palm – my God.

I reached the end of what I could do for his torso and his face, and he still hadn't stirred. I bent down and tugged his shoes off and wriggled him out of his pants, and then folded them over his hips like a loincloth for propriety's sake as I finished washing the rest of him. He seemed to be sleeping more easily now – and wounds that I'd washed once looked better when I looked at them again.

Only I knew it wasn't my makeshift washcloth doing that.

I stared at a laceration on the inside of his upper arm, one of the many bites he'd received. I'd just shoved the meat of it back where it'd belonged, a wedge of muscle and skin the size of a silver dollar – and it was knitting back together, slowly. There were scars, but the wounds themselves were closing like they'd never been there at all. I leaned forward, determined to watch him healing in slow-motion like he was a science experiment.

My necklace swung forward as I did, free from my sweater after all my tossing and turning last night, and it landed on his chest. A second later I heard a sizzling sound and saw black streaks trailing away from it. The locket itself was teetering, as blisters began beneath. He whined in his sleep, shuddering it away just as I snatched it back up – it'd left a perfectly burned oval on him, a charred black spot over his heart.

I looked from the locket – unharmed – to him, with a scar the size of a thumbprint.

Whatever Max was...wasn't normal. But it didn't change what he'd done, did it? He'd risked himself, for me – for Vincent. I concentrated on that and finished washing him up, with my locket hidden inside my sweater again.

Two hours later, all of his lacerations looked closed. I'd washed most of the blood off. I set the washrag aside and tried shaking his shoulders.

"Max. Max – wake up."

His body lolled with the motions, but didn't move.

"Come on, Max. You're healed now, right?" I wondered if his mind was hurt in the fight, and if his body could also heal that – but he'd driven here, so his brain had to work, didn't it? "Max – hey –" I put one thumb on an eye-lid and pulled up. The eye underneath wasn't brown – it was golden. I gasped.

Before I could pull my hand away he moved faster than I could even see and bit me. Not hard, not yet – but human teeth held onto the side of my hand, and when I tried to pull away they bit harder.

"Max, it's me, Sammy, remember?" I said, my voice rising. "We're friends, Max. You know me." I didn't dare yank my hand back, I knew he could bite me faster than I could move. Inside his mouth his tongue licked back and forth across my hand – and his eyes opened as though he was awake, but they were still that golden-hue.

"Max," I said, breathing hard, scared.

He sat up slowly and I moved with him. It was like watching a horror movie where someone came back to life – only Max hadn't died, had he?

He freed my hand just as he took my wrist, still keeping me close. He licked my palm and it would have tickled under different, less ominous, circumstances. I tried to pull my hand back – and he growled at me, a completely animal sound coming from this throat. His naked chest rose and fell, and the loincloth I'd given him had fallen away with his rising erection.

"What are you doing?" I asked him, no longer expecting an answer. He pulled me close and one of his hands reached up into my hair and pulled it down, forcing me to show him my neck. He licked it like an animal would, broad strokes, tasting all of my skin, sending shivers up and down my spine. It was a raw feeling – like he'd just let himself go, and something *other* had taken over.

I knew what it was like to feel like that – I longed for it, for the sensation of release, of giving over to something else wild and implacable. His tongue ran up the underside of my jaw and I tried to move, to catch his mouth in mine, but he pulled my hair tighter, holding me back. I whined in complaint and he growled me into silence.

He pushed his face in at the collar of my sweater, breathing deeply, rolling both of us back, until I was pinned by him on the floor, him straddling me. His one hand kept my hair tight while the other roamed my body, pushing the sweater up. I felt my necklace skitter across my collarbone and thump onto the wooden floor behind me, as his mouth came down to suck and bite, tasting me with almost more pressure than I could bear. Without thinking, I reached for his heavy cock and felt him shudder as I took hold. I clawed my other hand down his back as hard as I could, knowing I couldn't hurt him, and heard him – whoever *he* was now – rumble deep inside his chest.

He reached down between my legs and pressed two fingers into me. I gasped and arched, still stroking him as he brought his fingers to his mouth to taste them, his golden eyes on mine. My breath panted in his time – I wanted more, now, I wanted to spread myself wide for him, to let him take me, for us to rut like the animals we were. An inhuman sound escaped my throat, a whine, begging, pleading, as I pulled one more time on his cock, and – he blinked, and his eyes were brown, and full of surprise.

"Oh – Christ," he cursed, looking down at me – then he threw himself to one side, like I was a grenade. "I'm so sorry – so, so, sorry," he crawled backwards, all prior sureness gone. "I didn't – are you okay?" he asked, eyes wide with panic.

I nodded, sitting up and pushing my sweater down. "Yeah. You?"

"Yeah." He nodded repeatedly. "I think so," he said, then passed out.

12

ammy-smell-good.

    Yes.

Almost-alpha!

I know. Something had changed in my wolf during our battle with Syd. We'd almost won, despite what'd come after, and both of us knew it. We'd had a chance.

Healing!

Yes.

Sammy smells like blood.

Smells like us.

I know.

Close now, washing – like tongues lick.

I relaxed into her ministrations, staying under the surface. The way she washed each part of me, and her gasps of concern – how long had it been since anyone cared for me?

Want like food, my wolf whined. *Need like fuck.*

No.

Want. Want want want.

Wolves were supposed to always listen, when man-skin was out. But so close to the full moon and me being so weak – *No!* – I protested, as my wolf took control of my body. I could only feel things through its senses now.

Neck exposed. So soft, so easy to hurt.

Salt of sweat tastes sweet.

Scent of her like musk – push muzzle between her legs and l.i.c.k – need Sammy, want Sammy, mount Sammy –

I could feel our cock, hard and swollen, and if he used it on her like this – I fought through with the last of my strength and took control again, banishing my wolf back inside me.

I looked out our eyes and saw her spread out beneath me, my hand tangled in her hair tight, feel her hand on my cock, and smell her readiness in the air. "Christ –" I leapt away from her before I could do anything stupid.

"I'm so sorry." How was I going to explain that to her? In addition to everything else? "I didn't – are you okay?"

"Yeah. Are you?"

I nodded. And then my eyelids felt heavy again and I was drawn back to sleep.

WHEN I WOKE UP, the sun was low outside. I sat up. There was a coat on top of me, and the fire was still stoked – but there were a line of traps between me and the side of the room where Sam sat, watching me.

"So this is how it's going to be?" I couldn't blame her. My damn wolf –

One of her eyebrows rose. "I didn't know who I'd get when you woke up – Dr. Jekyll or Mr. Hyde."

"You have no idea how sorry I am about that."

"Uh-huh," she said. "Keep talking."

There was no way to hide from it now, I owed her an explanation – forty of them.

"I'm a werewolf. I was hurt, so my wolf took over for a bit there – it wanted to mount you. I'm completely mortified." I was careful to look at the traps near her feet instead of meeting her eyes.

There was a long pause before she asked, "Is that a compliment?"

I nodded. "I think so, at least. He's never come out like that before, with anyone. But I've never been that hurt before, either."

"What the hell hurt you?"

No reason to hold anything back now. "Other weres. I went to a bar last night to get answers, and got into trouble instead." I finally dared to look up, and found her calmly watching me. "You're taking all this rather well."

She licked her lips before speaking. "Vincent had a tattoo of a wolf paw over his heart. When I asked him about it, he'd only say that it was old. Between you and him and the burn my silver locket gave you," she pointed at a scarred spot on my chest. "I kinda figured it out. But I wanted you to be the one to say it first, because I knew that it'd sound crazy."

I nodded, because yeah, it did. "I am so sorry –"

She swatted my apology away. "You told him when you were with him, didn't you."

It wasn't a question.

"He saw me heal one day, I had to – it didn't make him love me any less." He didn't think I was a monster – even if I almost had been with her – I put my head in my hands.

"It's okay. Honestly."

Was it? My wolf could scent her earlier – and I could smell her now. She'd been as eager as my wolf was – but she didn't know what she was getting into. It wasn't safe. "When did he give you the necklace?"

"When things started going south. I couldn't see it at the time, 'cause we were in it, but," her hand rested on the locket. "He told me never to open it, unless he'd died."

"What was inside?" I was momentarily jealous of her for still having some small piece of him.

She tilted her head, and her hair swept over one shoulder. "Your phone number."

I sat there stunned as she stood and crossed over the room to me, stepping carefully over the traps to sit down just out of arm's reach, my sweater riding up her thighs. Vincent knew this might happen, that she might need me – and that I'd always be here waiting for him. "Did you find anything out?"

"Syd was supposed to be guarding him that night. He wasn't there, and I'd bet money he tipped the Caminos off."

"Syd?" she asked, her voice rising. "He's a werewolf too?"

"The pack alpha. Theoretically, my boss. What he says, goes." I shook my head.

"He's in the book." She flipped to his page instantly and handed it over to me. I scanned the page – some of the dollar amounts on there were huge. And the list of names – I recognized a few of them, from my time in the game. I had no doubt they were people that Syd had murdered.

"Who else is in there?" Was I?

Sam frowned and flipped through a few more pages. "Do you know JD, and Georgie?"

I slowly nodded. "How did you know?"

"They're all dog-earred. Which I bet Vincent thought was hilarious when he was doing it." She gave me a sad half smile. "Was your whole pack in on it? I mean, he was going to turn them in –"

"Along with half of the rest of the family," I said, trying to make apologies for my kind, while putting a horrified hand to my mouth. I was the reason he'd died. Without me, they never would have ingratiated themselves, they'd still be living from season to season, off the land and construction jobs.

"What's wrong?"

"It's all my fault," I said. "I'm the reason he's gone."

She tilted her head at me. It was a gesture Vincent had made with me a thousand times, and seeing her make it hurt me deep inside. "How?" she asked.

I inhaled deeply. "It wasn't until I got involved with Vincent that Syd realized the weres could work for the family. If I hadn't been with him, Syd never would have taken my place."

I waited for her to yell or cry or go. I wouldn't stop her – I had no hold on her, no matter how my wolf felt. Instead she stared at me, quiet.

"One night I did one of those jealous things, and asked him about who he'd been with before me," she said, breaking the silence. "And he told me a story about you."

I froze, waiting for the next words to fall from her lips.

"He said there'd been someone in his life who meant the world to him – and that lies had torn them apart. I'd assumed it was a woman and I never asked to hear the rest, I didn't want to, but," she said, as I swallowed, watching her. "He told me other stories, too. About his bodyguard before Syd. How you saved his life, more than once. I remember his face – it wasn't the kind of face you made about someone like Syd." Her voice was soft and kind. "In retrospect, it was pretty clear he hated Syd – we both did. He's kind of an asshole."

"Yeah." Vincent had saved a part of his heart for me after all. I thrilled to hear it, even as it made missing him that much harder.

"He made it clear he wouldn't have lived as long as he had without you. So I have you to thank for that. And you never did anything to hurt him – other than go."

I closed my eyes. How many times had I wished I'd been strong or stupid enough to stay with him then and take on the whole pack, rules and danger be damned? Would I have been happier dying alongside him that night? After seven years of living in the hills, the answer for me was yes.

But my going had kept Vincent alive – and she'd gone on to make him happy, without me. I flipped to the front of the book again, with its invocation for her safety. "I've got to get you away from here, Sam. You and the book – he wanted you both safe."

She reared back. "No way. We're not done yet. Now that we know Vincent's death is Syd's fault – I want revenge."

I started shaking my head. She needed to go. "It's not as simple as that."

"Because he's your alpha?"

"Because he's as indestructible as me. And the rest of my pack – they hate me."

"Why?"

"Because what I am is not allowed."

Her eyebrows rose. "And that is?"

"Bi." I looked away from her. "I like guys as much as I like girls." I remembered when I'd realized it too, when I'd been stumbling drunk out of a bar I wasn't old enough to be in. Hal had hauled me out into the alley to beat sense into me – weres couldn't risk getting jailed, what if you were in prison on a full moon night? – and cracked my head against the bricks. I sank down to my knees, seeing double for a minute, reaching up to beg forgiveness, finding myself on a level with his cock.

For one decisive moment, Hal stared down as I stared up, and then after that both of us knew what we were going to do.

He unzipped his pants and pulled his cock out and I took it in my mouth, hot and hard, feeling his fingers twine in my hair as he fucked my face. I let him, dropping my jaw down as far as it would go, taking him deep inside my throat, feeling the bulb of his head bobbing at the back of me. A minute, minute-and-a-half later, Hal was gasping above and I was swallowing cum.

He looked down at me, shoving his dick back into his pants. "Tell anyone, and you'll die."

I shook my head. I wouldn't. I was just as hard as he'd been – and the second he left the alley, my hands were all over my cock until I came.

Hal wanted more, eventually taking me into the forest, teaching me how to use my ass to pleasure him. He – and then others – took me front and back, and I was foolish enough to think that it made me special, that I was loved, even as I jerked myself off afterwards, completely alone.

"And they don't like that, why?"

I blinked myself back to the present. "Because only a wolf with a mate can be an alpha – and wolves don't mate, male to male." I knew you could show another man your knot, but it that didn't count. My wolf loved Vincent's alpha-nature, but it'd never tried to mate him. Not like it just had with her. "They used me until I was smart enough to realize that they hated me. And then I stayed out of their way, until Vincent made me his man. Then the pack edged in and pushed me out –"

"And that's when Vincent found me," she said.

"Yeah. And I came here. To hide and lick my wounds."

Her hands played at the edge of her sweater. "Did you hope that he'd come back to you?"

"Of course. Even as I knew if he did they'd kill us both. And I still wound up getting him...." I folded in on myself in blame.

"I thought you were going to die Max," she said, cutting me off. "You should've seen yourself. There were holes, bites, everywhere. I can't believe that you're alive."

"Me either, really," I said quietly. I remembered enough of the fight to know that I should have been dead – and that I was winning, before the others came in.

Almost-alpha! my wolf howled, in triumph.

I'd challenged Syd and then my pack arrived. Once they'd hauled me outside some of them had changed into wolves and bitten me – I put a hand to my throat, remembering the feel of teeth *twisting*.

Only the fact that I hadn't changed into a wolf had saved me, and the old rules about weres not killing other weres. If I had changed, my life would have been forfeit, fights as wolves ended as them. But it was perfectly okay however, to screw other weres over, literally and figuratively, and to set up people that they loved.

"I saw you Max, you should've died," she said, with an emphasis on the *should*. "But you didn't. You're alive for a reason."

Almost-alpha, my wolf agreed with her. She crawled over to me, and inside my wolf's tail beat low at seeing her on all fours.

"It wasn't your fault, Max," she said, taking my hand. The neck of my sweater hung open on her, showing me her breasts and the swinging silver locket. "It was Syd's – and the reason you're still alive is so that we can make him pay."

Was it?

God, I hoped so.

. . .

SHE WANTED REVENGE – and I wanted her. She was mesmerizing, electric. I couldn't take my eyes off of her and hidden underneath my coat my cock ached. I moved to the closet to pull myself out jeans and wasn't sure if I wanted her to turn around as I put them on or not – I wound up turning my back to her, wondering what kind of boundaries we had now, if any.

When I came back to join her by the fire, I did my best to act normal as we figured out our plan together – and I tried to figure out how to tell her certain truths alone.

"You're sure you can get all the traps set in time?" she asked me as she stood up to heat the kettle. My sweater barely covered her ass. My wolf whined, and I forced myself to concentrate.

"Yeah. If you can get us the silver. The guns...." I shook my head. That was her plan. She said it'd work but I wasn't so sure.

"Trust me," she said, with a wicked smile.

"All right." I couldn't help but.

First thing tomorrow, after a real bath in the creek, we were going to buy silver and shells – revenge would require luck and a large quantity of ammunition. But it was late now, and I could see the exhaustion of the past few days resting on her, around her shoulders and beneath her eyes. I stood, making my way across the room to take the couch, while she pulled herself onto my sheetless mattress. Without talking about it we'd agreed to go into our separate corners for the night.

But there was one last thing. I inhaled and exhaled deeply. "We have to take the moon into account."

"That's all we've thought of this whole time, Max," she said, her voice thick with sleep. We'd planned everything to happen when the pack and I would be trapped as wolves, underneath the full moon's glare. That way the pack would have to stay up here, and it would be safe in town for Sam to meet the Marshall.

"No," I said softly. "On me." I couldn't ask it of her. And yet I had to. I was glad that the bed was closer to the fire than the couch, so that I could see her, but she couldn't see all of me. "Only a wolf with a mate can be alpha, Sam."

"So?"

"Only an alpha can defeat Syd."

"You don't think silver buckshot'll do the trick?"

"That's assuming he falls for everything. Some of the others will – but he's smart."

"Yeah, I know. I used to try to give him the slip sometimes." She snorted. "So – well – mate me."

Inside, me, my wolf howled in triumph – and I slapped it down. "You don't know what you're saying."

"We fucked the other night, Max –"

"Mating's different. It's deeper than that. It's not just fucking."

"Realllllllly." Her tone was bemused.

"It's a connection – it's –"

"How many people have you done it with before?"

"No one."

"Not even Vincent?"

"My wolf doesn't work like that. I'm bisexual, but my wolf – well, it'll take what it's given, but it wants a woman." *It wants you,* is what I couldn't bring myself to say.

"Then how do you know what mating's like, if you're a virgin?"

I groaned. "I know what I know, all right? If I mate with you, there's no going back. It'll be like challenging Syd directly. He'll do anything he can after that to kill me – and you."

"They're already hunting me," she said, making everything sound logical. "Besides, how do you even know it'll work, since I'm not a werewolf too?"

"I just do." My wolf knew he would take her – and that *it* would take.

"Why're you so scared of it then?" she asked.

"Because," I said, unwilling to admit the truth. That mating was forever, at least for me.

"We can't have secrets Max. Not if this is going to work. If Vincent taught me anything, it was that." She sat up in bed, shaking her head.

"It's not just sex, Sam."

"Are you trying to tell me that it's some mystical magical forever thing?" she asked with a forced laugh.

"No. I'm trying to tell you that the reason I haven't done it before is I can only do it once. With just one person." I inhaled deeply and steeled myself to tell her everything. "I don't know what'll happen on your side, honestly. I just know that once I mate you, that's it for me."

A long silence passed between us as I saw her shoulders straighten. "You're kidding."

"Not in the least."

"And...you want that...with me?" she asked hesitantly. A piece of wood broke in the stove and made a crackling sound, while fresh light poured through the stove's grates to shine on her, letting me see her more clearly – the outline of her high breasts beneath my sweater, her angular legs tucked beside her, the way she was frowning at me with her intelligent eyes.

I'd only known her for a handful of days, and I'd already found her beautiful, fierce, and strong. No wonder Vincent had loved her. And maybe this was why he'd sent her to me. Not just to protect her, but *for* me.

"It's not a matter of want," I told her, my voice low. "It's a matter of need."

She shivered – either in fear, or at the honesty in my voice, I didn't know. "What if I don't feel the same way afterwards?"

"Then you go."

"And, what, leave you broken?" she protested.

"Don't worry about that. I've been broken before." It was my turn to laugh cruelly.

I heard her swallow before asking, "Are you really willing to risk everything on a chance at revenge?"

"Yes."

But it wasn't just that anymore, was it? It was on a chance at being with her. Mated. For life. I'd already spent seven years eaten up by regret for a path I hadn't taken. I wasn't going to let a second chance at happiness go.

Not even if I had to kill for it.

Not even if it killed me.

I could almost hear her thinking as she breathed quietly. "Okay. Tell me how you want it to go down."

I hadn't even begun to let myself hope that she'd agree – I wasn't sure I'd heard the words, even as she said them.

"You must have thought about it before," she said, taking my disbelief for hesitance. She lay back down on the mattress but rolled over so that her whole body was facing me, her curves a wave my hands wanted to ride. "So why not tell me what I'm in for?"

I leaned back into the couch. "It has to be under the moonlight."

"Go figure," she teased. I watched silently her from the darkness, being as implacable as I could be, waiting her out until she bowed her head. "Sorry."

"Don't apologize. But – I am serious, Sammy. Because you were right before. You need to hear everything. No secrets now." I watched her nod and restarted. "I'd want you naked in the woods by the time the moon rose over the trees. You'd go into the forest, until you found a glade – and I would follow you there as a wolf, finding you by your scent, until I saw you there in the near dark."

I'd imagined what it would be like, before, back when I'd been young enough to still have foolish dreams. I knew exactly what I wanted, what my wolf needed, to feel complete.

"Keep going," she quietly urged me.

"I'd want to rub against you, feel your fingers stroke my fur, breathe all of you in – before I changed into a man."

Her hand on her hip carelessly bunched up my sweater, exposing more of her thigh as I talked. Did she know that I could see her? Did she care? "I'd want you on all fours, just as I had been earlier. I'd want you to turn and suck on me. But what you won't realize is how hard I will be trying not to gag, how much I'll want to make you take it deep for me, to feel my balls slap against your chin with every thrust. I'll want to take you, Sammy. And when the mating comes on me, I won't want to hear no."

I paused, worried I'd gone too far, but I could hear her breathing, soft and fast, and smell her, oh God, smell her – everything about her was intoxicating, and my wolf whined. *Mount her now,* my wolf begged, our erection growing hard.

And that was the problem.

"But it won't be just be me. It'll be my wolf, too. We'll be sharing my body – and I may not be able to control everything that he'll do."

"Like what?" she asked, her voice low.

Like what I wanted to do to her right now? The same as my wolf wanted earlier? *L.i.c.k.*

"He just – he's rough. He used to come out more – when I was in fights. He hasn't gotten to come out in a long while."

"But I thought with the moon –"

"I mean come out inside me. Under the surface. Like he was when I woke up earlier – he's an animal, Sam. It's not safe for you."

"Tell me how to make it safe then."

"There is no way to make it safe." When my wolf took over it was an animal – when it was hungry, when its cock was hard. "Do whatever I say. Try to stay calm. Don't run. If you get scared, show your neck and belly – submit."

She nodded. "Then what's next?" she pressed. I saw her hand drop lower, fingers sliding in between her thighs and she had to know that I could see her, smell her. She made an intoxicating sound. "We don't have to pretend, do we?" she asked, lifting her top leg slightly up.

My hand reached for the front of my jeans, to rub myself, then hesitated.

"Max – if this is what you need – what we need," she said, her words hanging. I watched her hand rub herself in lazy circles and listened to her moan before she spoke again. "Then you can take me. I'll do whatever you say. I'll be good."

The scent of her wetness hung in the air like some rare perfume – and I unzipped quickly, pulling myself out.

"I know you want me. And I know I want you. That's all we need to know," she said, pushing her fingers inside herself and rocking forward to ride on them, watching me.

"You don't get it," I said, starting to stroke myself. "I'll have to fuck you so hard, Sam – you don't even know," I panted.

"So tell me," she whispered, going back to rubbing her clit. Her fingers were working faster now, and I wanted to kiss her there, to push my tongue inside her and taste her beauty.

"I'll pull my cock out of your mouth and walk behind you, and push you onto your legs again. And then I'll sheath myself in you, hilt deep." Images flashed in my mind. Teeth and claws – I imagined myself pushing her into the ground, and fucking her madly – and –

"More," she whispered.

"I –" stroked my cock desperately, losing concentration –

"More –" she demanded, for herself.

I imagined her taking it, pushing back against me, my knot stretching her wide. "And I'll fuck you," I promised her. "Like you were made to be fucked, like you were a were. I'll fill you with my cock, taking all of your pussy, fucking you madly until you howl out to the world that you're mine."

I came, hard, cum raining down on my belly, my knot flaring as I gasped. "Sam – come here."

She made a strangled noise. She hadn't come yet, and she needed to – but she needed to see me more.

"Now," I demanded. She straightened instantly, and pushed the sweater down like she'd been caught.

She crossed the room to me, and the smell of her sex, God – I kept stroking my fat cock, cum still dripping out of it. She eyed my hands – jealous of them? – and then gasped at what she saw. The way the base of my cock flared out, thick and wide.

"It's my knot – and it's why I'm afraid I'll hurt you. When I mate you you'll be locked to me for a time."

She pursed her lips. "I can handle that."

"You won't be able to get away from me. No matter what happens. No matter who I am – or what I do. You understand, right?" I needed her to fill in the blanks with her imagination. It was one thing for a were to bite another were, but to bite a human with were-strength –

"Yeah," she said with a curt nod. "I'll be fine."

I swallowed. It was what I and my wolf wanted to hear – but I knew she was lying.

Without her pussy wrapped around it, my knot was already subsiding. But if she let me, on that night – I wanted to take all the hope I'd felt earlier, rip it from my chest, and throw it into the fire to burn. Wanting to mate her, when she was a human, when she didn't even know me – what the fuck had I been thinking?

"So, um," she started, taking a step back.

"Yeah," I said gruffly. "Did you...?" I began. I didn't want to leave her unsatisfied, but I didn't even know if she'd let me touch her, much less mate her, now that I'd shown her all of me.

"No." She quickly shook her head. "It's late, and –"

"Yeah." I shoved myself back into my jeans and closed them.

She danced over the traps back to the other side of the room and tucked herself back onto my mattress. After a few moments of silence she said, "Goodnight, Max."

I hitched the coat higher so that it hid more of me. "Goodnight, Samantha."

13

What was I doing here?

Vincent had sent me to Max to be safe and instead – whatever we were doing here was the opposite.

I turned on the mattress to show him my back, tucking my arm underneath my head for a pillow.

I couldn't get revenge without him. I needed him.

But I wasn't prepared for him to need me.

Which was unfair, perhaps. I'd drained a lot of things out of a lot of men in my time – and most of them had never required anything back, just a warm welcoming hole. Vincent was the only man who'd broken the mold, who'd wanted more than just my body, who wanted to know me.

And now...this.

A werewolf. It sounded completely absurd. I should've asked him to change to prove it. But I knew what I'd seen on Vincent's chest – he'd had that paw-print tattoo since before he met me. No wonder Vincent had given me my necklace if silver did that to them.

Syd, JD, Georgie, Karl – the names on the dog-earred pages of the book haunted me. I knew them. I'd hung out with their girlfriends, drinking cocktails late into the night. And they'd all betrayed Vincent, to a man. To a wolf.

All of them had to pay. No matter what.

I'd bought plenty of things with my body before.

Vincent's revenge would just come with a higher price.

I WOKE up after dawn the next day and found Max still asleep. Maybe he was healing? I didn't know. I quietly rummaged in his closet until I found a clean pair of jeans and pulled them on. They hung so low on me, my hips barely wide enough to keep them up. Then I went over to the pile of cash to count it. Ten grand. It'd be enough – I'd make sure of it.

"Wake-up, sleepy-head," I said, and Max stirred. I realized watching him that he was acting for my sake – he'd wanted me to feel 'alone' in the cabin. Probably for long enough to run away, if I was going to.

He didn't know me.

"Bath time," I announced, and walked down to the creek.

THE COLD WATER had no problem taking away the blood I'd gotten on me the night before. It was bracing, and the water was moving more quickly today, some new spot of snow had thawed miles away – I could feel it surging against me, running across my nipples and playing in between my legs like hands. I stood there and let it buffet me, making me stronger, taking away things that were human and soft and freezing what was left of me so that I could follow through on my plan.

I returned to the cabin and put clothes back on and scrunched waves into my hair by the heat of the stove, as Max left to do his own ablutions. My hair was almost all the way dry by the time he got back – another of his attempts to let me go.

"You're sure about this?" he asked as he came back. I looked at him and saw all the worry he had for me in his face. Was it about today – or what was planned for tonight?

"Absolutely," I said, and stalked out the door.

THE FIRST PLACE we went to was the most dangerous – it was in town, and it involved silver. There were a chain of Silver Stores in the area and I needed to buy as many small sharp and pointy bits as I could, for us to load into shotgun shells later. The more penetrative power the better. I was the only one who could do this part – I got the feeling that just stepping into the store would make Max break out in hives.

I put my wig back on for it, so I'd look different than when the family'd seen me last, and spent a thousand dollars cash on an assortment of jagged bits and pieces, necklaces that we could break down, earrings that were projectiles all on their own, and yards and yards of silver chain, thick and thin. The women in there thought I was the Second Coming by the end of my shopping spree, and I hoped for their sake they worked on commission.

I hopped into the car carrying three non-descript bags.

"You get it?" he asked, not looking me in the eyes.

I nodded. "Yep. Onward."

He shook his head and looked out the truck's driver side window.

THE UPHOLSTERY in Max's truck was already so grungy, none of the bloodstains he'd left showed. I took the wig off once we got outside of town and I flipped the sunvisor down on the passenger side to inspect myself in its cracked mirror. I tied up my hair, half-up, half-down, like I was indecisively innocent, and smiled charmingly at myself. What I was about to do would be easier with makeup on, but maybe more authentic without.

He put the car in park outside the first gun shop. "And you're sure this'll work?"

"Trust me," I told him, opening up the door. I gave him a look, one of the ones I used to use on stage when I danced, dangerous and challenging, with just enough vulnerability to encourage men to try their luck. Then I waved and walked toward the door.

THE FIRST OF my fake IDs was in my pocket. I was Sarah, and her birthday was only a month off from my own – Vincent, again, thinking ahead for me.

The gunshop was on the rural side of town, we'd chosen it to start with, it seemed the most likely place for my gambit to work – and it was away from the family. Since most of them had rap sheets, they had to buy their guns out of other family member's trunks anyhow, whereas me, with my cash and my ID, could be legit-ish.

"Can I help you with anything, Miss?" A thin man stepped out from behind a row of camouflaged jackets. His 'Howdy, I'm Jim!' badge was pinned to his shirt, slightly skew. I smiled at him, full-bore. He didn't stand a chance.

"Hi, Jim," I said with a smile. "I'm looking for a Remington 870 Express." Max wanted me to get one slug-gun, and the rest shot guns. I figured I should try to get the most important one out here in the boonies, first.

His eyebrows rose as he took me in – both my request, and my body. "Can do. What for, if you don't mind me asking?"

"Home protection – land protection, really. I've seen a wild boar out, and I think it's time for a little bar-be-que."

He frowned and shook his head at the silliness of me. "Miss, wild boars are crazy sons of bitches – you shouldn't go after it alone."

"Oh I won't," I said, a little breathless, pleading my case. "I just want to be ready, in case it riles my dogs. My ex always took his Remington with him when he walked the land – then when he left, he took it, too. Left me Riley though. Great big German Shepherd. If only she were a little smarter – I'm worried she'll get into trouble, and I won't be able to help her."

He nodded, willing to grant that a shotgun might be useful if you were defending a dog from a boar. "You'd have to be a good shot. Shoot your dog with a slug-gun, and it's game over," he said, taking another stealthy look at my breasts.

I grinned at him earnestly, twisting my head to one side. "I'll practice. I don't have much else to do nowadays."

He snorted and pulled out a ledger from behind his countertop. "Well, sign right here, and then three days from now you can pick this baby up."

"Three days?" I said, my voice rising with disappointment.

"This is your first gun purchase I take it?" I could see myself through his eyes – I was a simple woman, just as he had suspected the second I walked through the door. I nodded, wide-eyed and innocent, to encourage his beliefs. "Well, that's how it goes, Miss."

I frowned. "I live past the interstate. I came here because I was driving through. There's stores way closer to my place – and they'll be easier for me to get back to, three days from now," I explained and then sighed in elaborate disappointment – not at him, but at myself, for being just *so* foolish. "I feel awful for wasting your time – I did want to buy it from here. You've been so helpful."

"It happens, Miss," he said. He shrugged his shoulders. I caught him looking again – and he knew I'd caught him, I saw his face start to redden.

"Sarah," I confessed to him, like I hadn't minded. I stretched one hand out and drummed my nails on the counter in thought and then looked at him, eyes full of promise. "You're sure there's no way you can change it...Jim?"

I saw his mouth part to deny me out of habit, and then him stop himself in hope, just as I came forward.

"If you're wondering what I think you're wondering," I said, as I planted both arms on the countertop, leaning over deeply. The sweater I was wearing had a low V, and from here I knew he could see that I wasn't wearing a bra. "The answer is yes. It's...been awhile." I let my eyes take on a fevered urgency.

I could see the outline of his erection growing underneath his sensible khaki pants. Then he took two big steps to the side and flipped a part of the countertop back. "Follow me."

We went down a short hallway into an office. I could've turned back at any time – he was the kind of man I could say no to, even halfway through, and he'd stop, I could tell, but he opened a door and I followed him inside.

We were in a small room with one wide desk, ten black and white TVs stacked on top of it. All the security camera feeds led here. I could even see Max, outside, sitting patiently inside his truck.

"We've gotta be fast, before my boss gets back –"

"Fast is how I like it," I said, giving him another look before I walked past him to put my hands on the front of the desk and tilt my ass towards him. He reached for Max's jeans on me and they practically fell down. I heard him gasped at the sight of so much skin – and then I heard a zipper.

Seconds later there was a condom wrapper on the table by my hands, and Jim was pounding wildly away at my pussy. I was once again selling myself – but this time for a cause.

"You like that?" he asked from behind.

I thought about the people that'd gotten Vincent killed, getting filled with silver buckshot.

"Yeah, Jim," I arched back into him and purred. "Yeah, I do."

MAX'S EYEBROWS rose as I came out of the gunshop, with the Remington in a case and fifty rounds of ammo under one arm. "Told you."

"Yeah," he said, as I tossed it in back, and we went to the next one on our map.

WE CANVASSED THE STATE. Not everyone fell for me – some of the stores had too much staff, or some of the men were so unused to getting hit on that they were completely oblivious, or they had happy wives – or maybe boyfriends! – at home, but fifteen stores later, we had eight guns. Three blow-jobs, three fucks, two handies, and Max's mood darkened with every stop. I'd even gotten one of the guns for free.

"Are men always this easy?"

"If they're lonely enough, yes. And I'll tell you a trade secret – almost all men are lonely." I slouched into the passenger seat, and we drove to the hardware store in silence.

"Was Vincent?" he asked me.

I glanced at him. "No. I made sure of that."

He inhaled, and wisely exhaled without saying anything else.

"I was a prostitute, Max." If he was going to mate me, he probably deserved to know.

He sat straighter and looked over at me. "Really?"

"Yeah."

"How did he – did you –"

"He was a client of mine. It's how we met." I toyed with the edge of the sweater, where a piece of the yarn was starting to fray. "I think after you he didn't want to date anyone who could hide anything from him – so he went for people whose problems were all on the table. Or the mattress." I snorted softly.

"How did that happen to you?" He sounded mystified – and sorry for me.

"Same way it happens to anyone." I shrugged off his concern, feeling some of my old armor coming back. "Bad luck, bad planning, wrong place wrong time. My parents had me late – by the time they died in a car accident, my grandparents were already gone. I went to foster care, it sucked, and then, well – I found out I could dance. I made good money dancing for a while, until my car was in an accident and I broke my leg. Basically, cars have it out for me."

"Good thing I have a truck," he interrupted.

I smiled, still looking down at my hands. "Yeah. So. A friend of mine did some escorting on the side, and once I healed up enough I did too. But then the recession hit, and –" I shrugged, leaving the rest to his imagination.

"I'm sorry," he said.

"Don't be. It got me to Vincent – and I don't regret a second of my time with him." I hazarded looking over at him. I expected to find pity, maybe even scorn, but saw sympathy instead.

"You do what you have to, to get by," he said, and I nodded.

"Yeah. Always."

14

Halfway through her story I found the strength to let her go.
Letting her use herself – letting her use me – after what she'd been through – I'd been thinking with my wolf's urges instead of my heart. It had to stop now, before the moon, while I was still in control.

I parked the truck and she helped me make the three trips up the ridge with all of our stuff, then looked at me and smiled. "What's next?"

I pitched my truck keys at her and she caught them without thinking. "Those are for you." I made my voice flat and unyielding, and her expression clouded instantly.

"What's wrong?"

I pointed at the bag she was carrying. "Take the rest of the money and the book and go. Call the Marshall and get the fuck out of my life."

"But –"

I gestured towards the door.

"I'm not leaving you! You can't make me!"

"I'm leaving you – and I can." I stood up to my full height, making myself seem bigger than I was, more menacing. "Take off, Sam."

"But we had a plan, and we have all these guns, and –"

"Go." I let shades of my wolf through, I could hear it in my voice, using its frustration with my man-skin side to color the tone I was using with her.

"But –" she protested.

"This is my place. And my fight. Go."

Her hands clenched in impotent fists. "None of those guys meant anything to me, Max – they didn't, I swear –"

"Go," I commanded again. My voice rumbled with authority, and I saw her take a step back toward the door, cowed. Some animal part of her knew that she should run.

"I can still be your mate – I know how to be true –"

"Go!" I shouted at her, half a roar, and started lunging for her like I was going to throw her out myself – or tear her in half and eat her organs.

She screamed instinctively and ran for the cabin's door. I closed it behind her, and leaned against it. "Fuck you, Max!" she shouted when she was safely outside. "We had a plan! We were a team!"

She beat her frustration out on the closed door, and I didn't dare answer her, no matter how much my wolf wanted to howl back.

AFTER I HEARD the truck race off, I felt like I could breathe.

I'd scared her away. My only chance at mating, gone. This was why I wasn't an alpha – clearly I was an idiot.

But I'd finally done the right thing. It would be cold comfort when I was getting torn into pieces tomorrow night, but it'd still be right. I kicked a bag of silver jewelry gently. There was no way I could kill all of them – but I was going to make damned sure that I didn't die alone. I reached into the bag from the hardware store, and pulled out gloves.

I wound the silver chains across the teeth of traps, tacking it into place with messy gobs of silver solder, two windows of my cabin broken out to create a cross breeze for ventilation's sake, and a respirator strapped tight across my face just in case.

Almost-alpha, my wolf whined.

Sorry, boy.

I lost myself in my work so that I could ignore what I'd just done.

15

I stormed down the ridge. After everything I'd done for him today – he didn't get to treat me like that. He was right, I'd take his shitty truck, I'd earned it, and I'd just go, drive for the horizon until I was almost out of gas. I didn't need some mountain man's revenge, I just needed the law.

I looked around his truck, at the seat cushions impregnated with his blood, and remembered the way he'd been when he'd gotten back, after risking his life for me and Vincent.

No. Fuck him, for ditching me. For judging me.

That was what it was, right? It had to be. He'd wanted me up until I'd told him the truth. Vincent had never judged me for what I'd done.

I pulled the truck into the outskirts of town, found a gas station, and tugged on my wig, in case anyone was around to see me make a phone call.

I refused to go to voicemail. By my third call in a row, I got some irritated sounding secretary.

"Yes?"

"Is Marshall Bren there?"

"Who's asking?"

"I'd rather tell him myself." The family had eyes and ears every-where, and were well versed in bribes.

"Fine. Hang on."

A man's voice came on the line. "This is Bren," he said, sounding curt.

How could I guarantee it was him? There was a long pause while my mind raced, thinking.

"Hello?" he prompted.

"Have there been any leads in the Vincent Depolo murder?"

"You'd have to ask homicide," he said, sounding as annoyed as the receptionist had. "Wait – how did you get this number?"

"How do you think I got it?"

His voice went low. "Someone told you to call."

"They did."

"Hang on." There was a rustling in the background, a desk drawer being opened and closed again. "How can I help you?"

"It's more me helping you. I have something I want to turn in."

"Might I suggest that you get the fuck out of town and then mail it to me, express?"

"I wish that were an option, but it's not." I felt better about talking to him now, though. No one who wanted to catch me or the book would try to send me away.

"You do understand how dangerous –"

"I do. Is it safe to talk?"

Another pause. "Yes."

"Tomorrow night. Meet me at Rider Plaza, at midnight."

"Daylight's safer."

"No, it's not."

"How will I know you?"

"You won't."

"How will you know me?"

"Easy. You'll be the one who looks like a cop." I hung up after that. There was a slim chance that the Marshall's phone was bugged, or that it was somehow tracing me – he'd be there, or not, and Max's plan would be in full swing. I trotted back to the truck and drove off.

·   ·   ·

I wound through country roads until I was almost out of gas and then fueled up again. I had to stay in town until tomorrow night to make the exchange – Max hadn't thought about that when he'd kicked me out, unless he'd meant for me to be smart and go far away before calling in. He should've known that I wasn't – or that anytime I was, my luck didn't hold.

One hand found the locket on my chest. I'd been lucky for seven years in a row. That was a lot longer than some people got. The girls I'd left behind at Ray's – I was sure half of them were dead of overdoses or had rap sheets as long as my arm.

Without thinking – or because I was thinking too hard – I'd come almost full circle around town, just as the sun began to set. I was only a few miles from the turn off to go back to the forest where Max was, trying to turn himself and the surrounding forest into a one-man army.

He didn't have a chance without me. I knew it. He never would have shown me what he was last night, if he hadn't felt compelled to – he'd been embarrassed afterwards, and like a bitch I'd let him be, because I was embarrassed too. He'd been forced to show me all of his secrets in the space of 72 hours, whereas I'd been holding all of mine in reserve. No wonder Vincent hated hiding things so much. It put the person being honest at a terrible disadvantage.

I stopped at an empty four way intersection that didn't have a light. The only car there, I let the truck idle while I thought, hard.

And then I turned right.

16

I put my odds at getting half of the pack out of commission with the spring-guns and the traps, which'd leave me four to fight on my own – including Syd.

Almost alpha! my wolf growled, making its opinion of Syd known.

Not anymore, I informed him. Not with Sam gone.

I'd finished soldering – I'd put the traps out tomorrow on the trails the pack was likely to take in, and then I'd bait them further with things that smelled like *her*. She'd walked around in my sweater long enough for it to have her musk and the pack already knew her scent. I hoped they'd be so eager to find her that they'd take risks – and the whole cabin smelled like her. If I left the front door open and blew out the stove they'd have to send someone in to check it out. I hammered in the nails that I'd spin out trip wire on tomorrow. Someone was getting a silver slug in them by the end of the night. Hopefully Syd.

As for the rest of the guns – I spent the next few hours pulling apart shotgun shells and reassembling them with bits of silver tossed in, while wearing gloves. They'd have to get blasted close, for the fragments to get past their fur and thick skin – but a wolf would have a hard time gnawing a deep splinter of silver out before it poisoned them. And if I was lucky and shot it someplace good and soft, like into their nose or eyes – well, the whole night was going to require a lot of luck.

When I next looked up the sun was down, and I could feel the moon's quiet pull, urging my fur-skin out. My wolf would like that too – to race around the forest, making himself known after the indignity I'd put him through today by chasing Sam off. He didn't understand rightness – he was, after all, an animal.

I stood up and felt my back pop and made my way out to the porch. The night was serene, like it'd been every night for the past seven years. Except for her smell, it was like she'd never been here.

I wished that there'd been another way, that I'd have been smart enough to think of one. I breathed in deep again and again, as if by scenting her and doing so, I could keep part of her inside of me.

And then – my wolf beat its tail, knowing her before I did.

Sam, we thought in unison.

Not old smells from behind us – but new fresh ones, carried in on the night's breeze.

She was here. For us. Knowing what that meant.

And yet –

My wolf whined and pulled inside of me, trying to get out or take control. I wrestled with it, just like Jacob did the Angel, except I lost.

Maybe on purpose.

My feet left the porch of their own accord and started walking into the forest. A quarter mile away I changed into all fours.

I FOUND the first tree as the moon began to rise. It smelled like her sex. I ran my cheek over it then, wanting to rub the smell of her into my fur.

The next tree, and the next – I galloped along on her trail, growing more excited with every step, every heartbeat thudding blood into my loins.

I saw her before she saw me – a pale goddess under the moon's dusky glow – and I leapt into the clearing where she was before I thought to stop myself. She whirled and covered her hand with her mouth so as not to scream.

I fought to sit there, chest heaving, muscles bunched. I knew we didn't want to scare her, she wasn't were, but my wolf's urges – he'd never been like this, I'd never felt him pull so hard before, so desperate to get out and *mount her.*

She took a tentative step toward us, then another, and whispered, "You're beautiful."

Was I? No one but other packmembers had ever seen me as a wolf before, and I'd never seen my wolf in a mirror. I fought to watch her as a man. Did she know what she was doing? Did she know what she was going to let us do?

My haunches tensed, ready to leap upon her and knock her to the ground and rut her –

Then she snapped her fingers by her thighs, like I was a lapdog. Bemused, my wolf trotted forward, instead of rolling her to the ground.

It wasn't too late, I could change into a man again and send her away.

But as I stood still beside her, two hundred pounds of muscle and fur, claws and fangs, I felt her put her hand atop my head. One finger traced the fur of an eyebrow and then she became more bold, stroking her whole hand over one ear.

I leaned into her, intoxicated by the contact. This was how it was supposed to happen. What it was supposed to be. She raked her fingers through the thicker fur of my back and I shivered bodily, then wound around her, leaning into her, seeking more of her touch.

And then I knew without knowing that the moon was above the treeline. I could feel its light land on me like another hand.

It was time.

I sat back again. If she ran now I couldn't promise anything, but if she chose to just turn around and walk away calmly, my wolf would understand. I could still make him.

But she looked up at the moon and then back down at me.

"It's okay, Max," she breathed, and inside my wolf took control.

We changed. Fur-skin in, man-skin out, I heard her gasp to watch the transition – but I wasn't in charge anymore. I could see what he was doing, smell, taste, touch it, but it was like I was in a glass box, unable to change the course.

This had happened before. I knew if I concentrated I could break the glass and take over – but that would ruin this for him. For us both. For all three of us, if this mating was to take, and make beating Syd a real thing. So I fought to control myself, just let go, and appreciate him appreciating her.

He stood in my skin, triumphant, looking out at her with his golden eyes. We were as naked as she was, and all our blood was rushing low to our shared cock.

He grabbed her and she gasped. His tongue wanted to taste all of her, so that she hid nothing from him – he licked from her collarbone out to her shoulder and felt her tremble under his hands like prey, delicious prey.

Don't run Sam, don't run –

She stilled and the moment passed. He drew his face along her skin, breathing her in deep, groping at her ass with one hand while the other brought her breast to his mouth roughly. After he licked them her nipples went hard, and he noticed this, too, licking over their pebbly roughness again and again, with the need of an animal, not a man. She wrapped her arms around his back and tried to kiss him, but he growled – kissing was not for wolves, even in human form.

I felt her tense. So far, we'd been rough, but growling was an inhuman sound, there was no way to pretend that it wasn't. Her hands fluttered in the air and then found our back again.

Just hold on. Everything will be all right if you just hold on, I wished I could tell her – wishing I was sure it wasn't a lie.

MY WOLF'S attention wandered down her body. We nuzzled the underside of her breasts, feeling the weight of them give, lapped across her stomach, holding her hips in place with strong hands.

Slowly, tasting every inch of skin along the way, we knelt in front of her and pushed her legs open, exposing herself to us.

It was the very center of her, what we had scented all this time, when we'd known we'd wanted to mount her, hard. Hands pressed up and pushed her thighs apart and we buried our face against her pussy.

"Oh, God," she breathed above us, rocking back. Her hands wound into our hair and pulled to stay upright as we licked and sucked, wanting to taste every drop of nectar she released. The noises we made would have been embarrassing if we weren't so hungry for her – and if she wasn't so hungry back.

"Oh, God," she whispered again, as our tongue parted her and pushed in. "Oh – yes, more," she murmured, as we sucked on her clit.

Our own cock was heavy on our thighs, achingly waiting, as her pussy began to swell, wetter than even we could lick away, and she started to pant and moan.

My wolf knew in his animal way that it was time and pulled back. She swayed over us, eyes glazed out in bliss – and then she looked down, at her juices covering our face, at the heaviness of our ready cock. She knew what we wanted and she wanted it too. One hand on our shoulder, she made her way down to all fours, still facing us.

She looked more like a wolf then, panting like she'd just run a race. I thought my wolf would spin her to take her there, ramming himself inside, God knew I wanted him too – but instead he lunged for her head and wound his hands in her wild hair.

He infrequently got control – but he was always inside me, watching. He knew how good making her mouth fuck our cock would feel.

He pulled her head down as he arched his hips up. Her lips found the head of our cock and let it push in. He whined then, thrusting up, and she kept her balance with her hands on our thighs as her head rocked back and forth with the power of his thrusts. Her tongue rubbed the bottom of our cock as he pushed himself into the back of her, using her hair to ride her face as we made wild sounds. She made noises too, choked whimpers and gasping, but my wolf didn't care – each time he slid almost all the way out, only to thrust back in, feeling her lips purse against our shaft while she sucked our head, hard, our balls swinging against her chin. Watching her, smelling her, the taste of her still on our tongue, feeling it as she sucked him – my wolf threw his head back and howled his pleasure to the night, before looking back down.

She was crouched in front of us, the curves of her pale body, her ass rounded like twin moons – he pushed her back off our cock and spun her around without ceremony.

We were ready to mate her.

17

I really hoped that I hadn't gotten naked and lost in the woods for nothing. Right now, the thought of being mated to a werewolf was substantially less frightening than wandering in circles all night. And I hadn't forgotten Max's warning about bears or mountain lions, either.

What if he'd already put the traps out? What if one of them got me?

"Hello?" I asked the forest, listening for any non-creepy response. "Max?"

Nothing. Except for more crickets.

I had an idea then. It felt silly, but – I reached between my legs and rubbed myself. I was clean, yes, but my pussy still had my scent. I dabbed it onto the bark of a tree, about the height of where I thought a wolf would be. They didn't teach things like this in girl scouts.

I kept feeling silly, but I marked every third or fourth tree, until I reached a glade just like the spot in Max's imagination. Lightning or fire had cleared a space, leaving a circle of trees surrounding short grasses and ferns. Even if Max didn't find me – here was as good a place as any to spend the night.

I stared up at the sky, wondering where the moon was – and if

Vincent was looking down. I couldn't believe that this was a betrayal of what we had when he'd sent me here himself. He might not have imagined it'd go down like this, but it had, because of his meddling.

I mean – I'd had sex with hundreds of guys. What was one more?

But that was selling Max short. He was different, not just werewolf different, but honorable. And understanding. After I'd calmed down I didn't think he'd sent me away out of disgust or condemnation – he'd genuinely wanted me to be safe.

Little did he know that safety was just never in the cards for me.

There was a rustling behind me. I turned just as a massive wolf leapt out, and I slapped my hand over my mouth to not scream.

I didn't know what I'd been expecting – but Max was hip height, and as long as I was tall. His fur was the color of smoke by moonlight, gray striped over black, and his eyes were that same golden hue I'd seen in the cabin. He sat down watching me and I fought to conquer all the primal things in me that said that I should run.

Once I had, I whispered, "You're beautiful."

Without thinking, I snapped my fingers by my thighs.

He came over then, trotting easily, each of his paws the size of my palm. I touched him tentatively, scared that what, I would scare him? I became more bold, feeling the way his fur gave beneath my touch, stroking it until I was raking my fingers against him, and he was winding against me, pushing me back. It was sensual in an odd way, feeling him claim me with his touch, watching the way his eyes closed in contentment with each stroke of my hand.

But then the moon shone overhead. It illuminated the entire glade and I looked up at it, magnificent and mysterious, like a gem hung there for the two of us, and then I looked back at him.

It was time.

I could feel my heart in my throat, racing as it beat, and wondered if his ears could hear it too. He looked up at me and then he changed. It looked so painful, the way he was and wasn't for a moment in between forms, everything pressed wrong, folding in, pushing out – and then he was in front of me as I'd seen him last night, all human and yet all wolf.

He started licking me. I didn't know what to do, if I should recip-rocate, I was scared of making him mad – but I knew Max was inside him somewhere – his hot tongue was leaving warm trails down my skin and then he licked my nipple and I gasped. He kept going, his hands taking hold of my ass, yanking me to him like he couldn't believe that I was real – and I reached for him without thinking, wanting to hold him, to kiss him back.

He growled as I went for him with my lips, and I stiffened. Max was there...but not in charge. He waited, and I knew in a very small way that he was waiting to see if I would run, if this night would go from fucking to bloodshed. I stilled myself, closing my eyes until the moment passed, and his tongue began to seek more of me out.

Lower and lower, and it was like each movement he made was dropping a hot stone deeper inside me, until I knew there was nowhere else for his tongue to go and he moved his hands so that he could spread me wide. I gasped as his tongue went for my pussy, and held onto his head and shoulders as he shamelessly sucked.

I swayed, rising up on tiptoes as all my blood rushed to my hips. I'd been a beast of need before and his tongue was turning me into one again now – I'd never had a man eat me out like this, so urgently, like he was dying of thirst and I was dripping wine.

Inside, I could feel my orgasm start to swell – if he kept that up, if he didn't stop – I made small cries to let him know that I was close, to beg him to continue – then he pulled back, leaving me bereft. I looked down at him, still panting, and saw his golden eyes watching me. Suddenly realizing just who I was with, I carefully let go of him.

I sank to the earth with the weight of need inside my hips, needing to hold onto something – and the second I landed, his hands were in my hair.

I knew as he pulled me to his hips that I should open wide – and I tasted his cock for the first time as it slid into my mouth and throat. He started thrusting into me, hard, and I made helpless noises because I was and because being helpless turned me on. Vincent had gotten that, he'd known when I wanted to be lifted up – and when I wanted to be beaten down. Now, as Max's howling wolf made me choke on his cock, was one of those times. I was blissfully helpless, there was nothing I could do – I let him use me, trying to hold onto his cock with my lips when he pulled it out, and taking it deep at the back of my throat when he shoved it back in.

And then he shoved me off of him entirely and spun me around.

I had a second to know what was happening before I felt him inside. His hands pushed me forward and down, ass up, as he slid his cock home.

I groaned at feeling him land and tried to rise up but he pushed me back down, leaning over me, his hands reaching for my breasts, kneading them hard. I felt the grass on the ground tickle me as I moved with each of his rapid short thrusts. His fingers raked down my back and I cried out, half in pain, half in pleasure. One of his hands grabbed my hair again and pulled back, yanking me up, making me move with him, pinning me on his cock until he released me, shoving me forward again.

I knew Max's wolf was an animal only rarely let out – and I got the feeling it wanted to do everything it wanted to, to utterly own me, before being trapped inside again.

So I gave myself over to it. I groaned and I shouted, feeling his hard cock with each wild thrust, him pull me up to lick my neck again before shoving me back down, hands braced against the earth to keep my ass steady as he beat into me with his hips, him reaching forward to grab my breasts and use them to haul me back with, pinning himself deep inside, where I could feel his cock almost twitching, aching for release. I was like a rag doll in his arms, over-come with the sensations and his need, unable to fight back or even help him, because I didn't know what was coming next – only that he – that his wolf – desperately needed to come.

I cried out again, a wild sound, and listened to it echo in the night, and he hauled me back up as I did so, licking up my shoulder to the nape of my neck where – he bit me.

Hard.

I yelped in pain and surprise and he instantly disentangled

himself from me with a whine. I sagged forward, my breathing raw, my body sore, pussy achingly empty.

That wasn't it – was it? I looked over my shoulder at Max, and saw him there, sitting back, still hard.

He'd hurt me – or his wolf had – and he'd put the brakes on everything. I could feel a trickle of warm blood seeping from the bite, down my back, and knew he'd gotten scared.

Silly wolf-man didn't know that I *liked* to get hurt.

I put my hands down to fall onto all fours again, and turned away from him, bowing my head low, submitting utterly.

"Max," I said, looking back over my shoulder and breathing roughly, "mate me."

He made a strangled sound, and surged forward to shove his cock back inside.

18

M ate-mate-mate – things deep inside my wolf thrummed with anticipation, satisfied only by feeling her take our cock, again and again.

The moon was high, as high as I was on her, fucking her with my wolf in control. It felt wild, better than I'd ever dreamed it could, like conceding everything to him had freed me in some essential way to just be physical, seeing, smelling, touching, tasting, the feel of increasing tension –

We rode her into the ground and pulled her back up by her hair, keeping her pussy wrapped around us as we thrust deep, groping her ass, clawing our fingers down her back, howling out our triumph – and her shouting out, too, the wild sounds of a woman getting fucked almost harder than she could stand.

And then, when I was as lost in the moment as my wolf was, he bit her.

She yelped and I smelled blood.

I surged forward inside my wolf to try to control him, and made him pull back.

No! he howled in protest, inside and out. *Mate!*

Not like this! I howled back at him, beating my hands on the inside of our skin. I needed to get back out, to save her –

Then she turned to look at us. I thought I'd see fear in her eyes, and if I did that would break me – instead she smiled, and she moved in front of us to be on all fours again, bending down to offer us herself again.

"Max," she said, "mate me."

I barely had time to get my cock into her before my knot flared.

She gasped, and I gasped. I'd never felt it swell inside someone else before. And now – and now – my wolf took over again, still pounding in, even though we were locked, stirring our fat cock inside of her. It felt so good – nothing had ever felt this good before – because – because –

I grabbed hold of her shoulders and pulled her back onto me, onto my lap, her knees on either side of mine, until she was pinned on me completely, presenting her to the moon like some kind of ritual sacrifice.

My mate, my mate, my mate, my wolf howled, as our cum jetted out, claiming her for the both of us. Nothing I'd done had ever felt like this before, so intense, so right. I snarled behind her, licking roughly up her neck, one arm wrapped round to grab her breast. She was mine, just like Vincent had wanted her to be, he knew that she could take it – *take me* – beast and all. He had given her to me like a gift from beyond the grave and I was going to spend the rest of my life claiming her and God help anyone who came between us – I howled again in triumph, still coming, my knotted cock twitching hard inside her, load after load spilling out. I pulled back and felt her follow, trapped, and then shoved myself deep inside her again, because it fucking felt so good. We were locked, she was mine. She belonged to me.

My howl faded from wolf to human and I grunted, thrusting one more time inside her for myself. I'd never come so hard before in my life. And the connection I felt with her now – I wrapped her in my arms and held her to my chest.

"Is it you again?" she asked softly.

I changed from holding her, to holding her up, trying to support more of her weight. "Yeah." The scent of our sex thick was in the air. We'd done it, we'd really done it, and I'd felt it take.

We were mated now. For life.

Or I was, at least. "Am I hurting you?" She shook her head and where her hair brushed against me it felt like fire. "Good." I wished I could see her face and read what she was thinking. Did she know? Did she feel this bond between us too? I wanted to lick at the blood on her back, but I didn't want to scare her with my strangeness.

"Actually, that was the least painful part of the process." She reached an arm up over her shoulder and wound it behind my head, possibly to touch me, possibly to just help herself hang on.

"What was the worst?" I murmured into her neck. "Getting bitten?"

"No. Deciding to come back up here. I was pretty pissed off."

"I bet." I sighed, breathing against her. I wanted to kiss her shoulders but while I knew my wolf thought she was ours, back as a human I didn't dare assume. She'd already given me so much tonight, it wouldn't be right to take more.

But I wanted to.

I wanted to cast an arm out and push the world outside away so that I could take her at my leisure. We'd fucked fast and desperately, but now I wanted to take my time. I wanted to explore her, all of her, underneath the moonlight.

I wanted to know her as a man. I stroked her hair back from her shoulder and felt her move against me again. The sensation sent shivers up and down my spine, my knot was still trapped inside her. "You're so tight," I whispered hoarsely.

"I know," she said, her voice just as rough. Then she started to squirm. I thought I'd pushed my luck too far, but she reached and took my hand from where it was over her chest and pulled it down, pushing it between her legs.

"Rub me?" she asked.

I paused, not daring to hope – nor press my advantage with her pinned on me.

"You feel so good, Max," she whispered, writhing on my swollen cock. "Touch me there."

I could hardly deny her when everything she wanted turned me on. I growled my pleasure in her ear, and listened to her moan. "Oh, Max," she said, as I kissed her neck at first softly, then harder. I wanted to know all of her now. I might not get another night.

She gasped and purred against me, pushing her back into my chest, as I played her like an instrument – running my thumb over the peaks of her nipples, my other hand's fingertips circling her clit, and me making the smallest of movements with my hips, testing the boundaries of her tolerance with my knot.

"It hurts so good Max," she said, tensing her ass to make her hips rock back and forth on my knot's width as I rubbed her. She started to clench me tighter and I growled. She was my mate, for eternity, and all of me knew it.

"Oh God," I groaned.

"What?" she asked, and then she felt it too, giving a soft moan. I was hard again, inside her. Her pussy had been too much. But I didn't want my wolf to come back – I started to panic –

"Just go with it, Max," she whispered, feeling me worry. "And whatever you do, don't stop."

So we writhed together quietly. Her hand went for mine and stopped my rubbing so that I could catch up. The smallest of movements either of us made were amplified by how sensitive I was and how tight all of she was around me, and we panted and moaned, our sounds mixing in with the cricketsong.

I was wrapped up in her, by her, it was like could feel my soul becoming entwined with hers, with each of my knot-trapped shallow thrusts. She was holding my cock, taking me, like she needed me, like I needed her to, and I knew she was mine. "Oh Max," she whispered, pushing my hand with hers, begging me to help her find release. I reached down and rubbed her in time with my strokes, felt her arch back against me, and watched her lift her breasts up, like she was presenting them to the moon, and then she shuddered in my arms.

"Max – Max – Max," she whispered, in time with my short

thrusts, and then the sensation of her pussy clamping down as it claimed me as I had her – she whimpered and cried out, her body rocking against mine in waves as she came. Her pussy enveloped my cock and rhythmically pulled, as I grabbed her waist and pulled her down, hard, grunting as my balls rose to shoot my second load of the night inside her.

"That's good Max, that's so good," she moaned as I sagged back, panting, empty. It was another ten minutes until my knot deflated, and until then she let me hold her quietly.

"Is it always like that?" she asked, breaking our silence as I slid out.

"I don't know. I'm a virgin, remember?"

"Not anymore." She stood first, shaky. She was as beautiful now as she had been earlier, even though the moon had sunk.

I'd claimed her. I really had. My wolf beat its tail in pleasure. She was ours.

For at least one more day.

I picked her up and carried her back to the cabin, putting her gently onto the bed. I made her let me clean her, my cum from between her thighs, and the blood that'd tracked down her back, and she was asleep – really asleep – by the time I came back with her clothes and the truck. I'd used the corner of her sweater to carefully pick up the silver necklace and nestle it into the bundle of her clothing.

Half of the woods smelled like her – the other half smelled of us, together, the dark scent of our sex.

The pack would come tomorrow night.

I looked around the cabin, at the traps I'd prepped and the silver-laced buckshot I'd readied.

Let them.

19

I woke up alone in the cabin again. Half the traps I'd seen in stacks last night were gone. I knew what Max was out doing.

I was naked and sore in all the best possible ways. Last night had been like some kind of dream. Him as a wolf, and all that came after. I'd never been used like that before, not even by Vincent. I ran my hands up and down my body, tracing the paths Max had made. Would Vincent have begrudged me this?

He would've wanted me to be safe – yes. He loved me, and I loved him. And he'd be all sorts of mad that I wouldn't let Max get rid of me, no matter how nobly he tried – because above all else, I knew Vincent wanted me to live.

But...Vincent also knew me. Knew my proclivities – because he'd cultivated most of them. I snorted, looking up at the cabin's low ceiling. He'd have known that I'd need someone who could handle me. Someone who could take my history at face value and not judge. Someone who wouldn't be threatened by the place Vincent held in my past.

Max was the only man who could do all three – and then some.

And after last night, he was the only man I wanted.

I'd felt bound to him, and not just physically, but someplace deeper, down in my soul. I was safe with him. Even when his wolf had bitten me. I knew he'd never let me get hurt again – except for in all the ways that I wanted *only him* to hurt me.

The part of me that always been struggling to feel seen and survive since my parents died – the same part of me that being with Vincent had calmed, and that'd had erupted back up after his death like a volcano – was quieting, safe anew with this strange man.

Max wanted to know me. And he'd shown me all of him.

I stood and tried to look over my shoulder at my back and ass to where I knew red lines and palm marks would stand out as the cabin's door opened.

Max was there, dawn's light coming in behind him like a halo. He saw me, brightened, and then saw my back and looked down. "I didn't mean to be so –"

"Don't apologize." I shook my head quickly. "This is me. This is... what I like."

His eyes measured me, trying to see if I was telling him what he wanted instead of the truth.

"You knew Vincent was a man with interesting tastes." I crossed the room to him slowly. "He and I –" I took his hand and brought it up to touch my breast, his hand fitting perfectly over a welt. While I searched for words, his thumb stroked across my nipple, and I gasped.

"Are you saying you're used to men treating you poorly?" he asked, his gaze serious and dark.

"No. I'm trying to tell you that I like to get hurt," I said.

His expression was a complicated thing, trapped between utter despair and elation. Then he pinched my nipple, pulling it up and towards him as he did so, making me rock toward him on both feet. A long moment passed between us, him watching my face for any sign of fear or hesitance, before he let go. Sensation flooded back, making everything my nipple felt sharp.

"All right." He bowed his head. "But know that I don't ever want to hurt-hurt you, Sam."

"Then don't die tonight." The words came to my tongue and

flowed out of my mouth before I could stop them. Everything was still for a moment, both of us frozen by what I'd said. And then he leaned forward and his mouth was on mine and his hands were on my waist.

He picked me up and threw me onto the bed, pulling off his clothes as he stood beside it, looking down at me, his chest heaving. I could see the outline of his cock beneath his denim before he freed it, and I spread my legs to take him – we didn't have time for foreplay, not when we were racing the moon. He mounted the bed, moving assuredly between my thighs, matching his body to mine, to meet my lips with his as he rocked up with his cock.

My hands wound in his hair, kissing him fervently as he thrust in. I was sore from the night before and it didn't matter – I was wet in moments, and he was free to fuck me like I needed him to. I wrapped my legs around his waist and pulled his chest down onto mine, wanting to feel every inch of his skin pressed close. He stroked all the way in and groaned my name into my ear, it made me shiver. The muscles of his arms, the broad sweep of his shoulders – I ran my hands everywhere, I had so little time to memorize him, but I had to – "Please," I whispered, more to myself than to him, and he stopped.

"Please what?" he asked, his expression open.

Please don't die, was what I wanted to say. But I didn't dare. One moment of vulnerability a day was enough – "Please – more –" I whispered, and he complied.

He grabbed my hands and set them over my head so I couldn't get away, and thrust in earnest, rocking his hips as he did so, leaning just enough over me so that I could grind my clit on his stomach as my hips answered his. The blood was rushing in my ears and I tried to fight back – not him, but all my memories, everything and everyway this could go wrong, after losing Vincent, I couldn't lose him, too –

One of his hands let go of mine and he used it to grab my jaw as his hips stilled. I blinked back tears as he made me look up.

"Stay with me, Sam," he said. "If this is the last –"

"Don't say that," I said, rising up to bite his lips quiet. "Don't ever say that," I begged him. I let my head fall back, tasting blood.

He let go of my wrists and held himself up with one arm, while the thumb on his free hand gently stroked over my bottom lip, wiping his blood away.

"I need you, Max," I admitted.

"For now," he said, his eyes searching mine.

I knew what I wanted to say, and it was insane, and foolish, and crazy – just like me. "For forever." I ran my hands up into his hair, my turn to make him look at me. "You took me like no one ever has, Max. Like no one ever could. You're my mate now. Which means you have to come back to me. Promise it."

He lowered himself over me, onto his elbows, covering me with his entire body. "I'm not in the habit of making promises I can't keep, Samantha."

"I don't care." My hands curled into impotent fists atop his shoulders. "I may not have a knot, but you're locked to me now."

One of his rough hands stroked hair away from my cheek. His hips started to thrust in time with his words. "I swear to you, Samantha – for however long I have – I'm yours – and you're mine. I claim you, Samantha," he said, with a rough thrust, his body barely hovering over mine now, his breath hot in my ear. "You're my mate now, and I'll never want another."

I could hear the truth in his words and it made it hard to breathe. "I don't want anyone else, Max," I swore to him. "Not ever again. Just you. Only you."

HE GROWLED, and my body took over. I started rocking with him, prolonging the contact between my pussy and his cock, and it was like we were dancing on the bed, moving as one, friction building inside and out. This was how it was supposed to be. I could feel it – and I knew he could too. My hands grabbed at him and I whined his name.

"Sam," he groaned in warning. "I'm going to –"

"Knot me again, Max – I can take it," I promised, grinding myself against him wildly.

His lips found mine and kissed me hard, before bowing his head near my ear. "You're my mate, my fucking mate," he snarled, and grunted, shoving himself deep inside. I felt the jerking of his cock as he came and gasped his name as I felt his knot swell inside me. My hands clawed his shoulders as he spread me thick and deep, feeling myself stretched all over again, deliciously sore from the prior night.

"Oh Max –" I moaned and he growled and kept fucking me, rubbing his hips against me hard until I came around him and beneath him in a series of gasps and shivers.

At the end of it I lay under him, trapped, his sweat dripping onto me, mine dripping onto his mattress. I moved a little – and he moved with me, his cock sealing us tight.

"Are you okay?" he asked, holding himself up over me with his well-muscled arms.

I nodded. I linked my feet behind his waist, since there was nowhere else to go.

He gave me a half-smile. "It's a little embarrassing. Sorry."

"Or, charming. I mean, I've seen some dicks in my day, but I can genuinely say that yours is something else." I tried to give him a cheerful smile back, but was hard to ignore that every second that passed now was one less we had to prepare.

"I know," he said, answering a question I hadn't asked. "I'm worried too." He rolled over a little and I went with him, until we were side by side, one of my legs tossed over his hips. He put an arm out for my head to rest on and smoothed away a wrinkle on my forehead with his free hand. "And I'm going to be really pissed that I found you now, if I don't get to fuck you senseless for the rest of my life."

I laughed for real. "Yeah. Me too." I leaned forward to kiss him and felt his body rock back against mine and it would've been nothing to twist and be on top of him and ride him like I wanted to – but. I pulled away from our kiss with a sigh. "You know, Vincent and I always had a back-up plan." Or rather, I thought we had a plan. "We always said if we got separated, we'd meet up at the Bica Museum coffee shop the next day. That we'd do anything we could to get down there in time."

Max shook his head. "Sam, you still need to get out of town –" he made a rumbling sound, half a growl, deep in his chest. "I'm only clearing out the pack. Not the family. If I live – you get out of town, and I'll call you."

"And, what, me just not know in the meantime?" I reared back, an action made harder by the fact that our hips were sealed. "The family isn't everywhere. They don't have eyes on every corner. I'll wear the wig –"

He reached for me, and pulled me close, burying me in him, his skin, his sweat, his scent. Whatever words I was going to say next were lost against his neck. He held me like he might never get to again, until his flaccid cock slipped out.

"Okay," he said, pushing back. "I have to go back –" he jerked his head toward the door.

"How can I help?" I asked as he stood. He reached into his jeans pocket and pulled out a closed knife, which he tossed to me.

"You can start cutting the top of that mattress into four by four squares."

I WORKED WHILE HE DID, leaving with bundles of traps over his shoulder, his pockets stuffed with things that smelled like me – like us. He said it'd infuriate the pack, and I believed him. I knew Syd's temper was dark, I'd seen him take it out on people often enough before.

Halfway through the day he returned and the cabin was empty, except for the few last guns he was going to set up in here. I knew it was time for me to go, but I didn't want to be the one to say it.

He stood in the doorway, the keys to the truck in his palm, offered out to me.

"These are for you."

By then I was wearing another outfit cobbled together from his clothes, a plaid flannel that swallowed me whole and jeans I'd been forced to create a belt for to keep up. I wanted nothing more than to take all of it off again and just be with him, one last time.

But instead I nodded, picked up my bag with the book, IDs, and cash, and walked up to him.

If I kissed him now, one or the other of us might break and lose resolve. I was his mate, because I was strong enough to be one, just like he was strong enough to be an alpha. And people like us – we did what we had to do, no matter what.

"The coffee shop. Tomorrow morning," I demanded as I took the keys from his hand.

I could see him considering fighting me, then give up. "All right. If I'm alive – I'll be there."

"You'd better be," I told him, then I carefully stepped around him and walked out before he could see me crying. I didn't have to look back to know that he was watching me, and that he knew.

20

She had to be the strongest woman I'd ever met – that I ever even knew. The way I could fuck her with abandon, the way her pussy clenched my cock – every moment in her presence made me hard. I would never tire of seeing her, tasting her, smelling her, touching her – and I was watching her walk away, scenting her tears in the air.

Almost-alpha, my wolf growled, our gaze following the sway of her hips.

That's right, I agreed with him. Back to business.

Tonight was going to work. It had to.

I HAD to do my thinking as a man and my construction around a wolf. How would the pack enter the forest? How many trails would they go down, into what groups would they divide? Could I lure some of them far enough away that no one would hear them get shot? What if they howled in pain – would the pack stop? Keep coming more slowly? Or faster, in anger?

I set traps, making sure some of them smelled like her and some of them didn't, hiding them among the low shrubs and leaf litter that scattered the forest floor. At strategic locations like the trail into the creek and back out again I mounted loaded shotguns, spinning out the thin tripwires that would set them off.

I'd rubbed fabric with her scent over so many trees – they'd have to know it was a trap after the first wolf got maimed or killed. But I knew just how angry my pack members were – they sharpened their anger like some men sharpened knives – and they all thought they were smarter than me, and smarter than one another too. I'd probably be able to kill three or four of them before they realized the danger they were in was real.

After that, though, it would require cunning.

I knew they'd wind up here. I nailed up boards over windows, so that the only way into or out of the cabin was the front door. And then I strung up trip wires for that, too, mounting shotguns to point across the doorway at wolf-height, and for one gun to point back out the door itself, hoping I would get whichever wolf'd hung back.

Then I mounted a third from the stove, I'd quenched its fire this morning.

If they made it through all the silver-poisoned traps and the silver-laced shotgun shells, I would be right here behind it, waiting for them.

IT WAS HARD NOT to test the wires again once I'd gotten all of the guns properly set up. Inside me, my wolf paced in circles, ready for his chance to be in charge. I was half-scared he'd go running after Sam, but knew he understood the gravity of becoming alpha, first. If we managed that – if somehow we killed Syd tonight – then after that, anything else was possible.

I paced across the small stretch of non-tripwired ground the cabin had left, until the light breaking through the boards over the windows faded and I felt the moon coming up.

Yes, my wolf hissed.

I changed, and then *he* was in charge.

· · ·

I was trapped in the glass room again, inside my wolf but not a part of him, not like the night before when we'd been sharing my body. He had the wisdom to sit on his haunches and breathed deep, listening for the pack. They usually came up as a group and parked their cars a few miles in before abandoning them for the change – wouldn't want a tourist coming across empty cars full of mysterious clothing in the dark. I knew they'd howl shortly though, their wolves triumphing at finally being in control again.

There. One lonely sound, instantly joined by others, all baying at the moon. None of them would even notice my absence – I usually only skulked in after a kill, to show my head and my fealty, strained as it was, to Syd. They would be stretching out, each wolf to his own devices as they started off through the forest, spreading out until someone scented something worth chasing down and called the others over.

This time, instead of a deer or a bear or a mountain lion, they'd scent *her* – and me.

And Syd would know.

Blood sunk into my balls just thinking about her, my wolf and I both aching for release. But we sat still and waited until –

One high sharp bark. The sound of a curious wolf. Georgie. I imagined him, his brindle fur blending in with the forest behind him, as he trotted down the southeastern trail I'd set up. It wouldn't be long now, if everything went according to plan –

A screeching sound of pain. Normal traps wouldn't hurt a were, but ones coated in silver would – and the more the wolf struggled, the more of the silver that'd rub against his skin. Blisters would rise and burst as the silver poisoned him – Georgie howled in anger and embarrassment, and then desperation as he realized the trap would be impossible to pull off. Silver would be coursing through his bloodstream – the others wouldn't be able to help him without also poisoning themselves, and none of them would have opposable thumbs until dawn. Judging from the sounds he was making, he didn't have that long.

I'd heard tell that silver poisoning was an awful way to go. My wolf looked down at our chest, where Sam's locket had scarred us, and mixed with the sounds Georgie was making now, we believed.

Other wolves picked up the sounds he made, sounding mournful and frustrated. And then one final long howl of warning. Syd's wolf, threatening me.

It'd begun.

NOW WE PACED. The safe width of the cabin was barely twice as long as we were, so we walked in tight circles, always listening, our sheathed cock swaying between our legs. The rest of my pack talked amongst themselves in the language of our kind, howls and barks – *come here, go there, scent this!, now!* – and I knew from being so intimate with our forest which scent they had found. JD howled in triumph at evading a trap – only to whine when the first of the spring-guns got him. The other wolves yipped in horror, and I imagined JD, seeds of poisonous silver boiling underneath his skin. He bayed like he was dying, because he was.

Part of me roiled at hearing his pain. The pack had been all I had for the majority of my life, except for my fleeting time with Vincent. But what had they ever done for me, once my propensities were known? Had they ever treated me with kindness since? And what they'd done to Vincent – what they wanted to do to Sam – a growl started low in our belly and it chased away all our doubt.

The woods went silent – no doubt as the other wolves spread out to more carefully look for me. JD had died.

Two down, seven to go.

Thirty minutes passed in silence. I had to assume they were being more careful now, canvassing the forest with more concern. They knew I was trapped in here as a wolf, just like them – and they wanted to reach me by dawn so that they would be allowed to tear me apart.

At last, sharp yips and howling in abject fear. A trap had gotten Mike – the howling was immediately cut off.

Had the silver really killed Mike that quickly?

My Ex-boyfriend's Werewolf Lover 165

Or had Syd torn out his throat to shut him up? Asserting himself before anyone could get scared and back down?

I assumed the latter was more likely.

Two gunshots, close together – whoever'd gotten shot going into the creek, had gotten shot again running back out of it before dying. Damn.

Four, I counted inside my wolf.

A high squeal from behind the cabin – someone'd been trying to circle around to surprise me, and a trap had gotten them.

Three.

Instead of howling, the last wolf growled. I'd know that sound anywhere. Karl.

The growling came closer, louder, more frustrated. He was in the clearing in front of the cabin now, sounding rabid. He clambered up the porch stairs slowly and I could see him by the moonlight, he had three paws free, and the last one was dragging a silver-covered trap. He lifted his lips and snarled at me, gnashing his teeth, daring me to come out and fight him.

Feelings in me surged, wanting to answer his anger with my own, to punish him for all the times he'd brutalized me in the past, the times he'd made me lick him low, but I held back as he came forward. He shambled into the cabin, going slower still as the poison burned him from the inside out, and I snarled –

In one final fuck you, Karl lunged, with the last of his strength – and set off two out of the three spring-guns.

Shit!

The rounds made his body jerk and spasm, but the shots were wasted, he was already dead.

My wolf howled out his frustration, and Syd's wolf chattered back from outside, taunting me.

Karl hadn't told Syd anything before he'd died, though – which meant my last trap was still in place. I stepped carefully on a piece of wood taped to hit a button on my phone, and Sam's voice came out of it.

"Is it over, Maxie?" a recording of her asked, breathless, frightened.

Syd's wolf appeared in the doorway. His eyes narrowed when he saw me, and he stepped in just as far as Karl had. No more – no less.

It didn't matter that he still had backup outside – if he figured out that Sam wasn't here – my wolf sprung into action, jumping over the final tripwire.

Syd reared up to meet me halfway. His teeth went for my throat but I twisted and smacked his jaws away with a forepaw, hard. His head twisted with the blow and came back up, snarling, teeth going for the side of my head, hoping to catch the soft part underneath my jaw or an eyesocket. I twisted to meet his teeth with mine, our fangs clashing together, I tasted the blood of a ripped tongue, and felt teeth penetrating my gums. We growled and snarled, causing one another even pain, and then he tried to push me back.

I knew where the tripwire was. I had to reverse our positions so that it was him moving backwards, not me. I reared back and spun around him, like I was aiming to clip his hamstrings with my teeth. He whirled, crouching low to give me less to aim for, and then it was his turn to be pressed back. He didn't want to give no matter how fast I harried him, snapping at his muzzle, neck, and feet. I had him on the defensive though – sooner or later, he would mess up – when he snarled again, this time a command, and Tony came through the open door behind my back.

I angled myself to try to hide my flank – it was clear from Tony's actions that he did not want to be here, his head was low, subservient, perhaps sensing that Syd's time would soon be at an end – but in the time it took for me to assess him, Syd had leapt back, and in one lucky move – the kind of luck that I never got – had missed the final tripwire entirely. Instead, his right rear paw fell onto the wooden stylus I'd used to operate the phone.

"Is it over, Maxie?" Sam asked again.

Syd stiffened, realizing my deception. And if Sam wasn't here – without a pack to lead he didn't need to fight me, as much as he needed to find her. He leapt for the open door past Tony, missing the goddamned tripwire yet again, racing off into the night.

Tony watched him go and then looked at me, plainly torn. I'd been besting Syd, and we three were the only wolves left. He could still side with his old master – or show fealty to his new one.

The way that it was always done was to show your belly and throat, exposing your most tender parts, a sign of utter trust.

Instead, Tony turned and sat down on all fours, curling his tail out of the way – offering to let me take him, as the others had taken me in the past.

I howled in irritation, and raced past him out the door.

21

At eleven thirty I put the truck in park and hopped out. The side street I'd parked on was bathed in moonlight. Was Max done fighting for his life? Had it worked? I wished the moon could give me a sign.

I pulled on my backpack, and walked over to the Rider park fence.

Rider Plaza was in the middle of the park. Family members weren't known for their appreciation of the outdoors, especially not past nightfall. They had streetcorners to run, clubs to bounce, whores to bully – which wasn't to say the plaza was safe. The dregs of town wound up here, people who weren't straight enough to get into a shelter for the night and those who preyed on them, scrabbling over one another's scraps.

I hunched over with my bag as the chain fence rattled too loudly behind me. The book was in the back pocket of Max's jeans, the folding knife in the front pocket, and both were covered by my sweater. If someone held me up, I'd gladly give them all the cash the bag held, but if they tried to get the book, they'd get cut for it.

With the moon out, navigating wasn't too hard – I'd chosen this back part because it was closest to the plaza as the crow flies. I saw a guy nodding off under a tree, and gave him a wide berth.

What was Max doing right now? I knew he knew the forest inside and out – but I'd seen what the pack had done to him, I couldn't not worry. One wrong step – hell, he could get shot by one of his own guns – the sound of someone getting beaten or roughly fucked inside a nearby grove startled me. I had to keep myself safe, for now. I cast one more glance up at the moon, and walked on.

The path was demarcated by sharp little metal posts that'd had their bronze caps stolen for scrap. I angled around a shadowed corner, and heard someone whisper. "What're you doing here?" and jumped back, landing softly. Recognized so soon? Shit, shit, shit – "What're you doing here, man, what're you doing here?"

I saw the speaker. He pawed at one ear like a dog and I realized he wasn't talking to me, yet. I made a wide circle, staying in the shadows of the trees on the path's other side until he was far behind.

The path widened until the plaza was visible. If it were a safer place, it'd have been gorgeous underneath the moonlight. I had no problem seeing the men and women huddled in sleeping bags and cardboard boxes, arranged in an oddly specific geometry around the perimeter. There was safety in numbers here, even if you didn't want anyone else to get too close.

I walked out to the fountain in the center, and sat down on its edge like I was waiting for a date, being watched by twenty sets of cautious eyes.

Seconds later I heard the click of a fearless heel atop cement. I wasn't sure what the difference between a cop and a marshall was – and Marshall Bren looked like a cop. Sharp shoulders, a paunch, and a general air of righteousness. Instincts from my former life rose up in me – how many times had I had to blow cops for free, so they wouldn't bust me? How many times had I been busted afterwards, just because they could? I grit my teeth, trapping words, and allowing no entry.

He sat down beside me, and spoke without preamble. "What on earth were you thinking, meeting here?"

I wasn't the only one who knew who he was – a few people got up and moved away, like they had other places to be at midnight. "How do I know you are who you say you are?"

He opened up a wallet and flashed me a badge plus ID. I'd never seen a Marshall's badge before – but if Vincent had trusted him – I nodded.

"You have it, right?"

I nodded again.

"On you? Can I see it?"

It was the only leverage I had. I stared at him, and he at me.

"I'm sorry about your man. He was trying to do some good at the end. I wish he'd come to us sooner – and that we'd been able to protect him."

His admission of culpability, right or wrong, was kind. And despite the fact that I knew as a cop he was using me with that kindness, I decided to share the book anyway. "Okay." I pulled it out of my pocket and handed it over.

He unsheathed a flashlight and bit its far end, so that the light beamed down onto each handscrawled page. It took all my strength not to hold onto the book's other side – I reached for my locket and chain instead. They were the only things I had left from Vincent now.

He thumbed through page after page, grunting. "Shit, yeah," he said around the flashlight. "This is perfect."

"You can use it? The whole thing?" I tried to be circumspect.

"A lot of people are going to be facing a lot of time, thanks to your man." He carefully put the book into a suit pocket.

"Good." I stood up, shouldering my bag.

Marshall Bren stood as well. "My chivalrous nature won't let me leave you here alone."

"I got in fine, I'll get out fine."

"I'm not worried about tonight. It's tomorrow, and the day after that – you're not going to be safe in town ever again. You need to come with me."

I took a step back. "I can't."

"You realize you're in danger, right? Or did you just get by this far on luck?"

"I know – but –" I couldn't go anywhere until I saw Max tomorrow morning.

Marshall Bren advanced a step. "The book's useless to me without you. They'll say we made everything up if we don't have you there to testify."

I shook my head – this was one reason we'd met in the park, so I'd have space to run. "I just need one more day –"

He growled. "I can't let you leave," he said, and he lunged for me. He caught me because I could see what was behind him.

A grey wolf appeared out of the park's shadows. It was the size of the Marshall, paunch and all. It came forward, limping, gobbets of meat visible on his right foreleg, and he started snarling at the sight of me.

I knew that it was Syd. It had to be.

Which meant that Max – something in my soul crumpled like a crushed can.

My jaw dropped in horror, and with his hand still firmly on my wrist, Bren turned.

To his credit, he put himself between me and the wolf, unholstering his gun with one hand. "Get back!" he commanded – me? Syd? – and he shot the wolf once, twice, but his bullets weren't tainted with silver.

Syd crouched, and I could see huge muscles bunching taut beneath his skin. He threw himself up into the air and it would've been so graceful to watch if it hadn't been meant to kill me. I screamed and cowered, dropping to the ground and throwing my arms overhead, expecting the worst, when I heard the sound of flesh impacting flesh, and fresh snarling.

I glanced up through my hands. A black wolf, out of nowhere.

"Max!"

Bren had control of his wits again, and fired three more shots.

"No!" I ran into him bodily, making him stumble against the fountain's cement side. He dropped the gun into the water, and started searching for it frantically, while simultaneously trying to push me back.

The water was dark, and he looked up at me. "Get out of here! Run!"

But I couldn't. All I could do was watch the wolves fight. The clouds moved again and moonlight shone down on the night's children. Max was standing between Syd and us, and there was a strip of flesh hanging from his cheek where Syd had almost popped his eye, and I could see red tears where teeth had raked through muscles on his haunch – while Syd favored one weak side, and I was guessing he'd yanked his foot out of a trap.

Max growled deeply, Syd barked defiance, and then they met again. Fur twined with fur, moving too fast for me to see who was winning, each pressing any advantage that they had, trying to kill the other one.

A high pitched squeak of pain. Max had one paw down trying to crush Syd's face – but Syd's teeth were latched into the thinnest part of Max's neck. One of Syd's eyeballs was hanging free, but his teeth – his teeth –

"No!" I shouted at the top of my lungs. I ran towards them, ripping Vincent's necklace off my neck. The locket went flying off the chain as I raced to Max's side. He made a strangled noise at me, his eyes wide, warning me away – Syd could've let go of him and killed me in that instant, I knew it – if only Syd could see me. But he couldn't and –

I wrapped my arms around his neck and lassoed the silver chain between them. Then I took the loose ends of my silver chain and pulled.

Syd hissed – either his mouth, or his neck, something hissed, it was a strange sound like a shaken nest of wasps. I pulled the chain tighter, and heard high, alien sounds of pain as I sawed the chain up, imagining it cutting through fur, skin, muscle, cartiliage. Warm fluids leaked out and covered me, like the center of a hundred blisters, and the scent of something foul burning rose.

Syd made one final sound and let go of Max's throat, whipping his head around, dislodging me, sending me spinning to one side. I could see the mess my silver garrote had made of his throat, where it'd sliced and burned deeply, and I didn't think the edges of any of his blackened skin would heal. He snapped at me. There was murder in his good eye, the other still bouncing against his gray-furred cheek – and Max bowled him over. He splayed Syd's jaw up with a paw, and reached in and bit the depth of his neck that my necklace had exposed. Carotids severed, and blood spilled out of Syd like oil, a slick spreading pool in the night. His chest took in two harsh breaths and then exhaled a final time.

Max's wolf turned to look at me. Beat to hell and limping and his golden eyes narrowed at something behind me –

The crack of a nearby gunshot. Marshall Bren. I whirled, hands to my ears, nearly deafened, as Max twisted and raced away.

"What the sweet fuck was that?" Bren shouted.

I put my hands on my knees and leaned over, dizzy. I felt like I was going to throw up as I lied. "I don't know."

WE WERE SWARMED AN INSTANT LATER. Bren hadn't come alone – he'd only pretended to, for my sake, but yeah, I should've known that no cop would come into Rider without back-up. They'd started running in with guns out the second they'd heard his first shot – the whole fight had happened so quickly and there was nothing to show for it.

Syd's body was gone. Not a wolf nor human remained. But I knew I'd watched him die – and there was a muddy pool of blood left behind, mixed in with splashing water from the fountain. No way anyone would get an uncontaminated sample now – and they wouldn't believe it if they did.

Just like no one would believe the rest of us. I played dumb and said I wasn't sure what I'd seen, only that I'd seen it, and how lucky was I that Bren was there to scare the bear-mountain-lion-monster off. And since the homeless witnesses they'd rounded up told even stranger tales, everyone was inclined to blow it off. Without a corpse, no harm, no foul.

But Bren knew – and he knew I knew. He'd question me later, alone, no doubt. I wasn't worried.

I wasn't the kind of girl who was easy to break.

AFTER THAT, I couldn't get away. I was rushed off to a safehouse on the outside of town. No one put anything past the family, not even hiring a killer dressed in a bearskin rug, apparently.

I had to admit I liked being back in civilization. Taking a shower that night and then laying down in a real bed – it suited me, as did a smattering of People magazines and late night TV.

But I didn't dare sleep. Not when I had to get out and make sure that Max was all right. Syd might not have been the last of them – what if he stumbled into one of his own traps, going back?

The officers watched me with a combination of disgust and pity. Even as I was willing to help them, I could see the natural penchant for hating snitches in their eyes. I'd played for the other team too long. I was untrustworthy.

But I was also just a woman, and I was also very tired, and I'd spent some time crying over Vincent really loudly in the bathroom, so loud that one of them came in to check on me while the other was off at the vending machine – let's just say it was a trick that Syd would never have fallen for, and I found myself outside a non-descript hotel just after dawn.

Without cash or keys it was going to take me awhile to hitchhike into the coffee shop, but as long as Max was waiting for me when I got there, I wouldn't mind.

I COULDN'T AFFORD to actually order coffee though, which made me feel like a heel. I'd bunned my hair up and I figured the generic clothes the Marshalls had given me to wear, ones that weren't covered in gore, would have to be disguise enough – it was worth the risk to be here.

I walked in and looked around. Everyone else was looking at their phones or staring into their coffee, waiting to wake up. I took a few more steps, trying not to look like I was getting into line because I wasn't, but –

"Sammy," a low familiar voice said. Hidden in an alcove by a cement pole, Max was lounging behind what looked like a latte.

"Hey," I said. My heart thrilled. We'd done it. We'd really done it.

"You alone?"

"For now. Probably not for long though." I sat down across from him, the cement post at my back.

He nodded. "That's good. I want them to keep a close eye on you. After this, you have to let them keep you safe. Promise me."

I opened my mouth to protest. I knew he was right, but I didn't care – I hadn't gone through all this just to leave him behind. I took the seat across from him.

"I killed the pack, not the family," he reminded me.

"I know." I looked into his eyes for answers. What were we now, other than strangers who'd spent the past week intensely? What did we have to talk about that wasn't the past? Did people like us ever get to have a future? "So are you king now, or what?"

The corner of his lips lifted in a rueful smile. "So to speak. Only one other wolf survived. Tony. I hate him."

I vaguely remembered knowing him. Some low-level grunt who wasn't smart enough to be involved in any plans.

"Is one follower a pack?"

He shook his head. "Not hardly."

"Then what's alpha without a pack?"

"Just a man." His voice was low and honest and I felt myself pulled like we had gravity – and I could see he felt it too. "I got you something." He leaned over and pulled a box out of a back pocket and handed it to me. I took it and slowly opened it up.

Inside there was a gold locket on a gold chain. I knew what I wanted to be inside the locket without opening it. "Is this what I think it is?"

"If you want it to be. Or it can just be a good luck charm – or you can sell it at the cash for gold place down the street." He watched me take it up with shaking hands. "Hope you don't mind that it's not silver."

"I don't," I said, fastening the clasp around my neck as he took back the box. His locket fell almost where Vincent's had, and I tucked it inside my shirt and pressed it against my chest with one hand. "Max – I don't know what's in store for me. They need me to testify that the book's real – and so many trials could take forever –"

His eyes searched mine. "I'm good at waiting. If you want me to, that is."

I knew what he was offering – was I brave enough to take it?

Who else knew what we'd been through? Who else had our shared history? I'd never find anyone else in the entire world like Max – or his wolf.

Vincent always knew what was best for me.

I nodded helplessly.

He stood up abruptly and pushed the table between us aside. It scraped on the ground and I was sure people turned to look but I didn't care – he stepped toward me as I stood up, and then the column was pressed against my back and he was kissing me, hard. One hand wound into my hair, the other pulled my hips close, and everything in me matched him, like we were meant to be together, like this was right. The way he held me, the way he smelled, the fierce intensity in his eyes before I closed mine and he kissed me, the way his lips covered me and his tongue moved against mine. He pulled back before I was ready and I sagged, held up in his strong arms, as he set his forehead against mine.

"Just wait till you're safe to call."

"I will. But I won't make you wait a second longer than you have to."

"Good," he growled, I felt it echo in my chest.

Someone began coughing pointedly behind us. Max's eyes glanced over, and his gaze darkened. I turned quickly – had the family found me out so soon?

But it was Marshall Bren, drumming his fingers on one thick thigh. "Samantha Carter are you, or are you not, coming with me?"

I gave him a sheepish look as Max subtly pushed me over. "Yeah, I am."

"Good. After you," he said, pointing to the patrol car parked illegally out front.

I looked back to Max. We'd already said everything we needed to say and more but – I put my hand to my chest where the locket was, and he smiled, wolfishly.

I turned around, fairly sure that I was grinning wolfishly too, and followed the Marshall out the door.

"DONE with whatever you had to do?" Bren asked, after settling himself in the driver side of his car.

"Yeah. I'll be good from here on out."

"Somehow I doubt that, but I'd appreciate you trying." He hit the gas, lurching us into traffic as he reached into a pocket of his sports coat. "I got this for you off of some homeless guy." He tossed me a plastic bag. It was Vincent's necklace, still discolored with gore and fur. I'd tried to inconspicuously look for it last night but I hadn't been able to find it – now I knew why.

Oh, Vincent, baby. I love you. I'll always love you. But the chain was broken and from here on out silver was going to be no good.

"Thanks, but I don't need it anymore." I handed it back to Bren.

"You sure?" he pressed. The sun was up now, blinding us both.

I flipped down the sunvisor and caught sight of Max's necklace glinting in dawn's light. "Yeah," I said, smiling up at my reflection. "I am."

MAX AND SAM'S EPILOGUES

S am's Epilogue:

THE TRIAL TOOK two long years. I did it for Vincent's sake, for his memory, even as I scratched every single lonely day out on a calendar.

I wanted to break, so many times, to pop open the locket and call the number I knew was waiting inside. The only thing that stopped me was knowing that I knew Max was waiting for me, too.

I knew he wouldn't stray.

And so some how I got by, muddling through my days, touching myself and thinking of him at night, until I'd given my last testimony and the government was done with me.

They offered to put me into a condo in a city, or a home out in the suburbs – but I asked them for a rustic cabin at the edge of a forest, and after I'd given them so many prosecutions they'd agreed. I signed a piece of paper promising I'd check in, and that I knew I could be under surveillance at any time, and the last officer I saw told me to make sure I stocked up on hair-dye, to keep my hair brown.

I waited until all of that was done, until I'd moved into the small cabin, and then I picked up the phone. My hands were shaking as I reached for the locket and finally cracked it open.

What if he didn't pick up? What if something had happened to him? I dialed the number, holding my breath – and three rings in he picked up.

"Who gave you this number?" he asked gruffly.

"You did," I said back.

There was silence on the other end of the line – I heard him breathing. He was alive, and so was I, and nothing was going to stop us, not ever again.

"Where?" he asked, more gently.

I gave him the address, and he hung up.

I SPENT the next morning in the woods behind my cabin.

I wasn't a fool – I knew the government had it bugged.

But I also knew that when Max got here – and he would come, as soon as possible – he'd be able to find me by my scent. And we could talk in the wilderness, safely. In the warmth of the sunlight, underneath the swaying trees.

I followed the main trail, and then I moved on to walk less used others, letting the terrain around me grow more wild until I found a place where I could sit and read on a fallen tree, with a water bottle at my side.

I could barely pay attention to the words, I think I read the same page three times – because mostly I was listening. For the sound of a snapped branch, a cleared throat – desperate for some sign of him.

He was quieter than I could've ever thought possible – I didn't hear him until he was ten feet away, and I didn't know how long he'd been there waiting, watching me, before I heard him quietly say, "Sam."

I looked up, startled, and the light was hitting him just right. He didn't look like he'd aged in the interim, he'd given his strong cheeks and jaw a clean shave, and his warm brown eyes looked at me with utter delight.

"Max," I whispered, standing up, book dropped.

And then we were running for each other. His hands picked me up and he swooped me around, and all I could do was kiss any part of him that I could reach, his face, his neck, his hair – just proving to myself, over and over again, that he was finally real.

He crushed me to him, I could feel his chest heaving, his strong arms wrapped around me, like he was never going to let me go again.

And I wanted to say everything then, I really did, to tell him how the last two years had been, how much I'd missed him, how hard it was – but looking up I knew I didn't have to. The way he looked at me, both hurt *and* hungry – it'd been just as bad for him.

I reached up and grabbed his head and brought his lips to mine.

His mouth opened and then engulfed me, threading his own hands through my newly-dark hair, holding me steady for the onslaught of his attention. His tongue swept through my mouth, claiming me, and I got to feel myself give in, for the first time in two years. I leaned into him and let him hold me.

I was with my man again.

My mate.

Max pulled back, to stare into my eyes. "I watched the news and read the papers. You were so fucking brave, and I was so scared for you."

I smiled up at him, feeling my lips start to swell from all his kisses. "You shouldn't have been. You told me to be safe. I'm good at doing what I've been told."

He grinned. "I don't seem to remember that from when I knew you."

"Shush. I stayed safe. I'm just sorry it took so long – but I had to do it."

"For Vincent's sake. I know." He nodded deeply, and I knew that he was the only one on earth who fully understood.

"And...you?" I asked, biting my lips as I looked up at him. He looked good. Was he?

Max set his forehead to mine. "I missed you," he rumbled. "Every morning, every night, and every moment in between."

I reached up and ran a hand through his hair. "You don't have to miss me anymore. I'm here. And I'm not going anywhere."

He turned his head into my palm to kiss it, and then licked across its skin. I yelped and giggled and he caught me up again, lifting me easily, looking at me as if he couldn't believe I was real – then his attention sobered, shifting into lust. I could feel my own body ready to answer as he asked, "Here?"

"Yeah," I whispered, reaching for the top buttons of my flannel.

"Fuck that," he said, grabbing for the fabric and pulling it apart. Buttons sprayed the glen like bullets, and he started kissing me fiercely, starting at my throat.

I wound my arms around his neck just trying to hold on. This was what I'd wanted, what I'd needed, what I'd craved – I knew I was already getting wet, as he wrapped me up and took me to the ground.

His mouth met my nipples in moments, sucking through the bra, before prying it up and off, me hissing as he first took them inside. I ran my hands up and down his back, the edges of his thighs, I made soft appreciative sounds, and I writhed.

Two years of not getting fucked, two years – *for a girl like me!* – of painful patience, obedience, and on-going trust. All this time a vibrator or a dildo, hadn't really been enough. I needed my man, my Max, so badly, and now I whined for him, yearning.

He growled, his tongue already lashing lower, his hands at the button of my jeans. He undid them quickly, and I raised my hips to help him pull them off, kicking off my shoes.

He positioned himself between my legs and lowered down to lick. One of my hands wound into the grass near my hip, and the other went for his hair. I felt his tongue part me and press me open, as his lips pulled at my clit but – "No, Max – later," I panted, squirming arching down to pull him up.

I saw the hunger in his eyes as they flashed up at me. "I just wanted to make sure you were ready."

I held myself up on my elbows in front of him. "I've been ready. This whole time."

He rose up on his knees in front of me, took off his jacket, and pulled off his t-shirt. His chest held the scars I remembered, and new ones that I knew he'd gotten, saving me. And then his hands dropped to the waist band of his jeans, undoing his belt, and pushing them down, to reveal the spectacular cock that for two years I'd only remembered my dreams. It swung down, as if drawn to me, and I lay back down, asking him to come follow me with open arms.

Max moved to hold himself above me, and then lowered all of himself at once, his muscular arms trapping me, his lips on my neck, the head of his hard-on slowly pushing inside. "If you can't take it – if I get too rough –" he warned in a growl.

"After two years, there's no such thing," I whispered, shaking my head.

He took me at my word and thrust, sheathing himself inside me.

I cried out. I was wet – but it'd been two years since I'd really been full.

And I knew he'd fill me more if we kept going.

"God," I hissed, just feeling the hard length of him inside me, all of my nerves stretched and pulled.

"You're perfect, Sam," he murmured against me, slowly pulling himself out. "You were made for me," he said, pushing himself back in. "We were meant to be together. Forever. Now. Just like this."

He rolled his hips, stroking in and out of me as he spoke, and I knew as he stared down at me that he meant every word. Floodgates I'd never known before opened between my legs and he gave another rumble as my juices slicked him, my body showing itself ready. He bowed his head and fucked me good.

I closed my eyes, my head rolled back, as he made me feel taken, again and again. He changed the angle of his hips so that the thick head of his cock dragged out of me roughly and he ground himself against me when he plunged back in, rubbing my clit with each of his thrusts.

I ran my hands down his back, feeling the muscles move there, and I curled up to kiss his shoulders and neck, until his lips caught mine and pinned me, his tongue taking my mouth just as fiercely as he was taking the rest of me, and two years of agony lifted away. I felt myself tightening – the muscles of my stomach tensing, my ass clenching my hips up, and the heat rising between my thighs as my pussy started to grab, like somehow if I only came hard enough, I would be sure to keep him here.

But I knew Max wasn't going to leave. I'd never be alone again.

And looking up at him, seeing him react to me and feel me, and know how I was building up – "Come for me, my mate," he growled, shoving his cock deep inside. He grabbed my breast, pulled a nipple, and it was just the right amount of rough. "Come for me so I can knot you and make you mine."

And at the thought of his cock taking me harder and spreading me wider, I cried out. The first shudder ripped through me, and then the second, and then a third, and then it was like I was on a wave that wouldn't stop. "Max, oh God, Max," I gasped, curling up.

He growled again and then grunted and thrust and I knew he was coming inside me. His knot flared and I moaned as I felt his thick cock pulse, filling me with cum. "Sam...Sam...." I saw his hands grab at the dirt near my shoulders and watched his jaw clench as his body shuddered, pleasure roiling through him and then out and into me.

Max cried out when he was done and dropped his body on top of mine, only barely holding himself up. There was a thin glaze of sweat between us, and the summer breeze made everything feel nicely cool.

He raised his head up slowly. "I knew I shouldn't have been worried," he said softly.

"But you were?" I finished for him.

"Two years is a long time," he said and swallowed.

"Shorter than seven."

He gave me a careful, open smile. "But you're human."

I put a finger on his lips. "No buts. I'm yours."

Max grabbed my hand, raised it to his lips to kiss, and for the first time in a long time, I felt happy.

MAX'S EPILOGUE

SAM REALLY WAS HERE – and I was knotted inside her, where I belonged. My wolf had practically howled when I'd come – fucking her had felt like coming home.

I kissed her hand and rubbed it against my cheek, covering myself in her scent – I'd never have to worry about anyone knowing she was mine again, from here on out.

She was beaming up at me. "Can I say something possibly stupid?" she asked.

I laughed, pushing myself up higher to give her space. "By all means."

"I think I love you." She scrunched her face up a little, nervous, like she was bracing for a blow.

"Oh, no, now I have to gnaw off my dick to get away."

Her eyes blinked open and saw I was teasing. "Shut up!" she said, shoving me lightly.

I laughed more and grabbed her hands, twisting them above her. "Why is that stupid?" I asked.

"Because," she said, thinking. "Two reasons. First off, I hardly know you Max."

"You know everything important about me. And we can work on all the rest."

"Let me finish," she said. "We'll start by working on your inter-rupting." I snorted, but waited for her to go on. "Secondly...it's just not anything I thought I'd ever get to feel again. Lust, yes, like, always, but...love? I just don't know if I trust that."

"You don't have to, then. Just trust me." I lowered myself over her, grabbed her, and wheeled myself onto the ground, so that she was straddling above me. "I won't ever let anything happen to you, Sam. Never again. The only times you get hurt from here on out are times when I know you want it." I surveyed her glorious naked body over me, still wearing her torn flannel, her freshly-dyed brunette hair wild with a few leaves and gossamer tangles.

She braced her hands on my chest, leaning forward, framing her breasts irresistibly. "You were worried about me being human, right?"

"Yeah."

"Well if I'm human and you're not...do you think you could love me?" Her eyes leveled with mine, searching me for the truth.

"Do I think I could love you," I repeated her softly with a sigh. "Samantha, I already do." She tensed at that – my revelation was clearly unexpected. "What do you think being a mate is?" I asked.

"I don't know," she said, with a headshake. "Not really."

"My wolf picked you. And I picked you. And I'm sorry you had to go, to be safe, to honor Vincent, and I never got a chance to show you." I rested my palms against her thighs. "But I'm here now, Sam, and I'm not going anywhere."

My knot subsided and I slipped out of her, as she leaned forward to cup my cheek with her hand. "I want to believe that so badly," she said.

"Then do."

"Vincent left me," she said, finally getting to the bottom of all her fears. The last time she'd loved it'd ended tragically.

"As much as I loved him, too, Sam – Vincent's not me." She rocked back and took a deep inhale, staring me down. "Come here," I told her, pulling her down to lay on my chest, wrapping her up in my arms. "I didn't wait for two years for you to be afraid of loving me, Samantha."

"Then you say it first," she murmured into my neck, and I could scent her tears. My wolf didn't understand how she could be happy and sad, both at the same time, it was too simple a creature – but I did.

I stroked a lock of her hair back, holding her close. "I love you."

I heard her swallow. "I love you, too," she said very softly.

"See?" I asked her, stroking comforting hands over her body. "The ice is broken. And next time won't be so scary."

She nodded her head against me, and then chastely kissed my neck.

Well, it would've been chaste, if she weren't naked, laying against my naked torso, with my jeans half down.

She kissed me again, and again, rising up in a line, until she met my jaw and kissed under it. I closed my eyes and let her move at her own pace, her hair brushing over me as she moved, like a paintbrush painting fire.

I inhaled and held it, not wanting to rush this for her – we'd already done fast, now it was time to do slow.

But already my blood was rushing lower, and my cock that'd so recently relaxed was starting to ramrod up again.

Her kisses continued until I couldn't stand it anymore, reaching up to run my fingers in her hair to bring her lips to mine. I licked a stripe across them, then left her yearning as they parted, so I could say, "I love you, Samantha."

She flushed red. My tough, streetwise, and occasionally violent mate – who I knew had a spine of steel – was blushing. I grinned at her and said it again. "And guess what? I still love you, now."

Sam made a face at that, and pushed herself up with her hands. "And what about now?" she asked archly, giving me a look.

I pretended to contemplate. "I...suppose so. Yes. This is still what loving you feels like." I nodded, like I was coming around to the idea, then I turned solemn. "I have two years without you to catch up on. You're going to have to get used to hearing it a lot...so you might as well start now."

She gasped at that, and brought the back of a hand up to wipe her eyes.

"I'm going to tell you, and I'm going to show you, and eventually you'll believe," I told her.

She nodded, sniffling a little. "It's hard."

"Only now. It won't be in time. I know it."

She smiled a little. "And your wolf knows it too?"

"He's known it longer, even."

Sam shook her head and looked around the forest we were in, as if seeing it for the first time. Free and happy. At long last.

We'd been chased by ghosts for long enough.

She returned her attention to me, staring down, and she was the most beautiful thing I'd ever seen. "I love you."

She laughed. "Okay you can stop now."

"Make me," I mock-growled. Her eyes glinted – I knew she took it as a challenge – as she bent over to kiss me, hard, making speech impossible. I growled again into her mouth, for real now, as urges surged through me. My heavy cock had been waiting patiently, but now – I took hold of her hips and pushed her back, as I arched my own hips forward.

She moaned as I parted her again, throwing her head back, as the head of my cock explored her. I kissed her breasts and her neck, and then I pushed her down my shaft.

All the wetness she'd had before was still waiting, and I sank in to my hilt with ease.

Yes. Mate-fuck-mate-Sammy, my wolf growled, laying just beneath my skin. It would never get tired of mounting her – and neither would I.

I grabbed her thighs and ground her against me, using her for my pleasure, while knowing that that was what she liked.

Giving over. Giving in.

Trusting – *loving* – someone enough to let it hurt.

I lifted one hand up and took a smack at her ass. She yelped and I felt the blow jostle her against me. She made a pleasingly helpless sound – and I did it again.

I alternated cheeks, while I pulled her on and off me, listening to her pant and whine, learning what she needed. I stroked her gently in between blows, cradling her to me, telling her how beautiful and brave she was, how perfect she would always be.

And all the while my hunger burned. It was like she was an engine built to turn me on. I couldn't get enough of her scent, of her taste, of her sound, and I needed to feel her come.

I braced my heels against the ground and started thrusting now in earnest, holding her still to take my cock. She liked that too though, just on the edge of being forced. Every time she whispered my name it made me harder, and her juices meant both of us were drenched. She dove a hand between us to touch her clit with more precision and at the thought of her desperately touching herself to come for me I growled.

"Oh, Max," she warned, and I felt her move, her body dancing as muscles tensed. I wound an arm about her waist and held her for me to fuck, while I wrapped the other in her hair, dragging her head down so I could whisper in her ear.

"I fucking love you, Samantha." It would always be easy to say, because it was true. "And I love fucking you."

She hissed once, twice, and then she moaned, and I made it reverberate with the ferocity of my thrusts. "Oh God, Max," she said, her voice raising up as she started to spasm. "I love you, too. I do, oh God – I do," she gasped, and then shuddered against me like she was falling apart.

I grunted and pushed my cock into the gloved squeeze of her swollen pussy a final time, and then I shouted as my knot flared out again. My balls lifted as my hips bucked, and I took her with me as I filled her up with cum, jetting myself inside, each spurt a separate wave of pleasure that was hers and mine alone. I kept groaning and thrusting until I was through, and then all that was left were tiny after twitches, like distant echoes of what'd happened returning, and the knowledge that my mate and I were still sealed tight.

"See?" I asked her, when I could breathe again. I ran my hands up and down her, and felt the heat rising from her ass from my smacks. I was going to have to take such good care of her, truly. I nuzzled my face against her hair.

"Yeah," she said, when she was capable of speech, rising just her head up to look at me. "I do."

"Get used to saying that, then," I told her.

Her eyebrows arched in a question and she smiled at me. "Why?"

"Because the next jewelry I'm buying you is a ring."

. . .

THANKS FOR READING Her Ex-boyfriend's Werewolf Lover! This book is one of my favorites, I hope you enjoyed it too! Please keep reading through for the introduction of Blood of the Pack: Dark Ink Tattoo Book One.

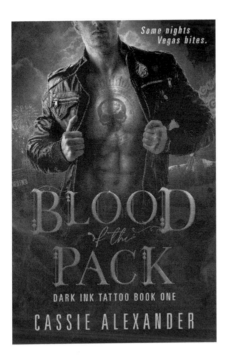

I heard an engine turn the corner, startled, and the MMA fighter I was touching up a truly regrettable tribal tattoo on yelped.

"Sorry. Spine," I apologized, peeking over his hulking shoulder to see Jack Stone arrive on time for work, possibly for the first time ever while in my employ. His black 1963 Lincoln Continental swooped through Dark Ink's parking lot like a hearse.

Just Jack. I knew what his car sounded like. Even though our shifts didn't overlap often – I'd heard it often enough to know it wasn't a bike. And still....

I sprayed my client's shoulder with cool water and wiped the blood away, trying to ignore the slight jitter in my hand. This was my job – this was my tattoo-shop – and I'd been doing tats for the past seven years in peace. I breathed deep and willed myself calm. I wasn't scared and I hadn't lost control, and if I kept telling myself that long enough eventually I might believe it.

I put the heel of my hand on the fighter's back to steady it and stepped on the pedal to get the gun roaring again, starting where I'd left off, cleaning up some cheaper artist's shoddy job. In no other profession was the phrase 'you get what you pay for' so true.

This time, the fighter twitched, not me. No way not to hit nerves when you were tattooing someone over bone. Tattoos on top of bone felt like you were getting stabbed.

A lot like getting menacing letters from your ex in prison.

FIVE MINUTES LATER, Jack was leaning over from the wrong side of the counter, purring my name. "Angela."

I didn't turn around. I knew where he was, of course, I'd just made it a habit to ignore him. Mostly.

"Hey, boss-lady, I'm on time, just like you asked," he tried again. I snorted, stopped working, and looked up.

A gaggle of barely-old-enough-to-be-in-the-shop girls flocked behind him, flipping through flash displays, clearly whispering to themselves about him. He was stare-worthy. If you were into tall, lean but muscular men, black hair, brown eyes, and full sleeve tattoos, Jack was your kind of guy. When our shifts overlapped I had to remind myself he was off limits the same way that ex-smokers have to remind themselves to forget about cigarettes. I knew it was for my own good – I'd quit men that were bad for me a long time ago – but that didn't make it any less hard.

It was also why I tried to ignore him. It was good for him sometimes.

"On time for once," I corrected him.

"It's winter," he said, like that was an explanation.

I saw the post office truck pull into the parking lot behind him and my stomach clenched. "Yeah, of course," I said without thinking, standing and pulling my gloves off. "Wrap him up, will you?" I said, sidling towards the hip-high swinging saloon door that divided our half of the shop from the client's.

"My pleasure," Jack said, setting his ass down on the piercing display case and spinning his legs over to switch sides. Normally I'd yell at him about that, but – I reached the door just as the postman did, opening it up to take our letters from him.

Junk mail, tattoo convention flyers, the electricity bill and – something stamped 'Approved by the LVMPD'.

Goddammit.

I bit my lips and ran for the office. I stopped myself from slamming the door, just barely, instead whirling to place my back against it, like that would help keep all the monsters at bay, and slowly sank to the floor.

I threw the rest of the mail to the ground and opened up Gray's letter.

Visit me.

Funny how it only took two words to blow my life apart. I bit the side of my hand to stop from screaming – but somewhere on the inside, a hidden part of me howled.

I tore his letter up – same as I'd torn the other three I'd gotten, starting two weeks ago, and threw the pieces of it into the trash. If only escaping Gray were so easy. I should've left years ago – given myself and Rabbit a head start – but then what? Keep running forever? When I knew Gray and the Pack would always be able to find us? No, instead I'd pretended that I'd had a normal life – that I was normal. I'd rolled the dice, praying that someone meaner and nastier than Gray would take him out in prison.

I should've known that no such person existed.

I'd lived in Vegas my whole life – you'd think by now I'd be a better gambler.

There was a quiet knock on the door behind me. "Boss-lady?" Jack's voice, full of concern.

I stood and straightened myself out, opening the door a crack. "I, uh, didn't know what to charge him – so I asked for two-fifty. That enough?" Jack asked.

It was way more than I'd have asked for. It was only a touch up, hadn't even taken an hour. "He paid that?"

"I can be very convincing," he said, and shrugged, searching what he could see of me with his expressive eyes.

"Stop that. If I wanted to tell you about it, I would."

He leaned forward and pressed the door open. I could've fought back – could've closed the door – but I didn't want to make a scene. But my office was meant for only one person, one desk, one chair, there was no way for us be in here and not be in one another's space. In other circumstances I'd thought about doing things to Jack in here that'd make even the most jaded local blush, but now – I'd much rather he hold me and lie to me that everything was going to be all right.

"What was that?" he said, jerking his chin at the other mail still littering the floor.

"Nothing."

He stared me down. Could he really read me? Or was he just one of those guys who made you think they could? The kind you had relationships with where you filled all the silences with too much hope?

"Seriously, Ang," he said, his voice low.

I gestured to include the entire parlor. "It all says it's for me."

"Even the one from the Las Vegas Metropolitan police department?" he asked. "Don't ask me how I know what stamped mail from prison looks like."

Damn, Jack being Jack. Too smart for his own good. "It's none of your business," I said, as boss-like as I could, shutting down the conversation.

Jack took his cue. "All right, all right,"

"And I need to go."

"Yeah, to your date, I know."

I hadn't told him I was going on a date tonight, that that was why I needed him to really-I-mean-it be on time for once. And he'd said it with almost precisely flat inflection, so I couldn't really tell if he was jealous or whatever – and it didn't matter, because I was with Mark now, anyhow. But some deep and secret part of me bared its teeth and wagged its tail.

He glanced down at the letters. "If anything bad comes of that, you let me know, okay?"

"Sure," I lied, and pushed past him, out the door.

IF YOU'D LIKE to read more, hit up Blood of the Pack: Dark Ink Tattoo Book One

IF YOU WANT to read more hot books – and who doesn't? – the best way to keep track of my fiction is to join my mailing list: mailing list.

AS ALWAYS, if you're happy, tell a friend – or tell the whole internet, and leave a review. These matter more than you know (plus encourage me to write more quickly.)

IF YOU'D LIKE to read some of my other hot fiction, my most up-to-date bibliography is here and below!

ALSO BY CASSIE ALEXANDER

Written with Kara Lockharte (and possibly as our co-author name, Cassie Lockharte):

The Prince of the Otherworlds Series – hot, sexy urban fantasy

Dragon Called

Dragon Destined

Dragon Fated

Dragon Mated

The Wardens of the Otherworlds Series – hot, sexy paranormal romance

Dragon's Captive

Wolf's Princess

Written as Cassie Alexander:

The Dark Ink Tattoo series – very, very hot paranormal romance

Blood of the Pack

Blood at Dusk

Blood at Midnight

Blood at Moonlight

Blood at Dawn

The House – a find your fantasy erotica

The House

Her Future Vampire Lover — futuristic vampire paranormal romance

Her Future Vampire Lover

Rough Ghost Lover — a sizzling paranormal erotica — DOES NOT HAVE HEA

Rough Ghost Lover

The Edie Spence urban fantasy series